AMERICAN GOTHIC

Robert Bloch

"His scene is Chicago at the time of the 1893 World's Fair, w [illegible] *Cairo where Lit* [illegible] *technical exhibi* [illegible] *tury's marvels,* [illegible] *telegraph. Near* [illegible] *pharmacist and* [illegible] *'sovereign reme* [illegible] *plaints,' built h* [illegible] *and the rooms he rented to Fair tourists. It was an intricate maze of hidden staircases and secret rooms where Gregg enticed his victims, young girls and wealthy women, willing and unwilling. Even the sophisticated reader will be gripped by the terror the Castle generates."*

PUBLISHERS' WEEKLY

About the Author

Robert Bloch is a prolific writer and over 400 of his short stories and articles have appeared in *Playboy, Hitchcock's Mystery Magazine, Ellery Queen's Mystery Magazine* and other publications. He also has nine films, fifty teleplays and several well known novels including *Psycho* and *Nightworld* to his credit. Mr. Bloch has received numerous awards for his work and was National President of the Mystery Writers of America in 1971. He and his wife live in Los Angeles.

AMERICAN GOTHIC

Robert Bloch

A STAR BOOK
published by
W. H. ALLEN

A Star Book
Published in 1975
by W. H. Allen & Co. Ltd.
A division of Howard & Wyndham Ltd.
44, Hill Street, London W1X 8LB

First published in Great Britain by
W. H. Allen & Co. Ltd. 1975

Printed in Great Britain by
Richard Clay (The Chaucer Press), Ltd., Bungay, Suffolk

ISBN 0 352 39813 2

This book is for
The Girls, Lil, Bee and Tess,
whom I've known and loved
longer than anyone else alive.

1

THE CASTLE stood in shadows.

Millie stared up at its towering turrets from the walk below as the carriage departed, clattering away across the cobblestones. And the castle stared back. Two eyes opened and glared down at her from the topmost turret.

"Pshaw!" Millie muttered. "They're only lights."

Of course that was what they were—any fool could see that—and there was no sense talking to herself. But as the echoing clop of hooves faded away into the night, the sound of her own voice was somehow reassuring.

She hadn't expected the street to be so dark, so deserted; she hadn't realized the castle was so huge.

As Millie crossed the walk to the entrance, she forced

herself to remember that this wasn't an actual castle but a brand-new 1893 building. The sprawling three-story structure with the false facade of turrets was only a make-believe, something out of a fairy tale for children. Real castles didn't have rooms to rent upstairs and a drugstore on the first floor.

There was no mistaking the pharmacy as she approached the display windows; the ornate glass containers loomed up from behind, filled with strange, shimmering amber and purple liquid. Only colored water—more make-believe.

But then, who was she to look down her nose at that? The rustle of her bombazine skirt reminded Millie that she was pretending too: beneath her dress, the bustle and padding and corseting were false. And despite the feathers, what she wore on her head was only a hat, not a broad-winged bird. In her hand she carried what was called a chatelaine bag—but she wasn't a chatelaine, a lady of the castle. Although she might be.

She *might be.* The thought made her heart pound; she fancied she could hear its thud mingling with the harsh clang of the pharmacy's night bell as she pressed the button beside the entrance.

Yes, she might be living in a castle, if the make-believe worked. The carefully contrived coiffure, the painstakingly applied powder and perfume and patchouli, designed to disguise thirty-five years of living beneath a mask of youth.

Sometimes it was hard to separate illusion from reality because you had to use one to attain the other. And even though you knew the difference between the truth and a lie, there were moments when it was best to pretend, even to yourself.

The sound of the bolt sliding back was real, and so was the grating of hinges as the door opened. The man who smiled out at her from the shadows was real too.

"Good evening, Millicent."

The voice was soft and rich and resonant. Just hearing it faintly over the crackling of the telephone wire earlier in the day had been enough to make her feel giddy, though she forced herself to answer calmly. And now she could scarcely speak.

"Gordon–"

She couldn't trust herself to say more, and she was grateful for the concealment of the shadows; he mustn't see that she was blushing like a silly schoolgirl. How absurd–a grown woman going all weak this way at the sight of her own husband! But he was so tall and so very handsome: even more handsome than she remembered, and she hadn't set eyes on him now for over–

"Three months," Gordon murmured. "Has it really been that long?" He shook his head. "How can you ever forgive me?"

Millie wanted to say that she'd already forgiven him, just as she always had over the years. But she reminded herself that she must be firm, so she merely nodded in reply. That was the way: use make-believe to attain reality.

"Do come in." He stepped back, and she moved across the threshold. He turned away behind her; in the darkness of the shop she heard the click of the bolt as the door closed. Then there was a bubbling hiss as the gas jet beside the door flared up, sending the shadows scuttling against the walls.

Millie stared, and Gordon smiled. "Well, what do you think?"

Millie controlled her voice with conscious effort. "It's very impressive."

And it was. The gleaming white-tiled countertops, the glass-guarded shelves lined with pharmaceutical preparations–everything looked so modern, so *scientific.* Trust

Gordon for that; he was such a stickler for the best and the finest.

Gordon nodded, pleased with her reaction. "Let me show you the rest of it."

As he led her down the aisle, she noted the display on the shelves behind the counters. Vin Vitae Tonic. Dr. Hammond's Nerve and Brain Pills. Dr. Worden's Female Pills. German Liquor Cure, Dr. Rose's Obesity Powders, Blackberry Balsam, Egyptian Pile Cure, Spirits of Turpentine, Parisian Depilatory, Worm Cakes, Petroleum Pomade, Sanitary Tooth Soap. All the latest discoveries of medical science, including the towering display of Electric Elixir, The Sovereign Remedy For Male And Female Complaints, Personally Prepared From The Secret Formula Of Dr. G. Gordon Gregg. Big brown bottles with white labels, each emblazoned with a handsome steel-engraved portrait of her husband, looking ever so dignified and impressive in pince-nez, as befitted an eminent physician and benefactor of humanity.

Again Millie reminded herself of the tangled skein, the mingling of illusion and reality. The pince-nez was make-believe; Gordon never wore spectacles, and the stern expression was foreign to his face. But he *was* a medical authority, and he had indeed labored for years to perfect his miraculous discovery. Time and again he'd come to her for funds in order to conduct research and experiments on Electric Elixir. She'd contributed from the savings dear Papa had left as part of the estate, and he had sacrificed so many nights of toil—working away from home in a secret laboratory he'd set up somewhere on the outskirts of the city. Even she had never known the location of that laboratory, nor did she know the ingredients of his remedy, but she did know the reality of its results. So many grateful patients had been cured; scores of ailing men and sickly women returned week after week to purchase fresh supplies of the Elixir. Millie herself had once tried the preparation when suffering from the painful cramping of female complaint; it tasted sweet, but a small amount made her dizzy and lightheaded, so she never repeated the dosage. Gordon told her it was the electric current that made it so strong; electricity was the life force itself, and compounding electric waves with healing medication had been a costly process.

"Consider it an investment," he told her. "An investment in the welfare of all mankind, and an investment in our own future. In due time it will be hailed as the medical marvel of the age."

Our future.

That's what Gordon had said. And that's what he always told her whenever she questioned his dedication to his work. All during this long last absence Millie had comforted herself with the thought of that future. Still, there were times when she sat alone in the house on Sunnyside Avenue, times when her hope had faltered. Those long, lonely nights in suburban Ravenswood: nights of waiting for a call that never came; nights of wondering whether Gordon would ever return. All she knew was that her husband was planning to enter business somewhere far across town, on the South Side; he hadn't even mentioned the address, and Chicago was such a big city.

And it was getting bigger now, spreading and sprawling daily in anticipation of the great event—the Columbian Exposition, the World's Fair. Millie had followed the stories in the paper, marveling at accounts of the huge complex rising up in Jackson Park. Burnham the architect was transforming five hundred and fifty acres of swampland into a dazzling domain of palaces and pleasure gardens, a wonderful White City. Would it be completed in time for the grand opening on the first of May? In late April the great nations of the world sent their navies to New York Harbor for review, and there was a gala military parade. A few days later, Chicago received the Duke of Veruga and Cristóbal Colón y Aguilera, descendant of Columbus himself. The Liberty Bell arrived from Philadelphia as part of the display, and there was a wonderful welcoming ceremony for President Cleveland.

The whole city seethed in expectation, and Millie was caught up in the excitement. But she didn't venture downtown for the preliminary pageantry; the crowds and cable cars were too much for a lady to confront unescorted. She read the news at home, alone.

And when the great day came she was still alone, though half of all Chicago fought its way to the fairgrounds that fine Monday noon to gather around the grandstand before the Administration Building. There were the glittering uniforms of the gold-braided dignitaries to goggle at; Theodore Thomas and his orchestra thundering forth the Columbian March; the invocation and prayer delivered by the blind clergyman Dr. Milburn. And then the President of the United States placed his hand upon the button and the Fair came alive. The fountains sprayed; the turbines throbbed; the electric lights blazed and bathed the wonderland with dazzling hues.

Electricity. Magic. The modern magic of 1893—a brave new world of telegraph and telephones, like the one Gordon had installed right there in the house on Sunnyside Avenue. A telephone that never rang. Until today.

Today, at noon, as the Fair was opening—that was when he had called. To tell her that his work too was completed;

that he was awaiting her presence at the address he gave her.

"I've built a castle," Gordon said.

And so she had come here, come out into that brave new world to see illusion transformed into reality.

Now Gordon was unlocking the door leading past the prescription department at the rear of the shop. Millie glanced inside as she followed him along the corridor, noting the mortar and pestle on the compounding counter and the contents of the shelves above. Pharmacopoeia. Vials and bottles and jars, in acrid, aromatic array. Liquid laudanum, spirits of niter, powdered opium, herbs and balsams and unguents, chemical concoctions. More magic—the magic of healing.

Just beyond, at the end of the hall, was another door. Gordon unlocked it, using the same key as before. He smiled at her from under his moustache, nodding in amusement at her puzzled reaction.

"One key for all," he said. "You'll see why in a moment." Gordon stepped aside, allowing her to move through the doorway, which, to her surprise, fronted a steep and narrow staircase leading up into darkness.

He turned on the gas jet flanking the stairs and motioned to her to precede him. "Mind the steps."

Millie lifted her skirts as she ascended, acutely aware that Gordon could see her ankles. Not exactly a refined gesture—but after all, they were man and wife. Her heart began to pound again, and it wasn't from the exertion of climbing the stairs.

"Here we are," said Gordon, behind her. And there they were indeed, on the second floor, where a carpeted corridor stretched off in either direction from the stairwell, lined with door after door on both sides of the hall.

"Lodging accommodations," Gordon told her, and held up his key. "You understand now why I need a skeleton key."

"But your guests—what about their privacy?"

"Their keys will open only a single door." Gordon turned up a gas jet, bathing the hall in flickering light. "Besides, I haven't any lodgers yet. This place was barely completed in time for the Fair. I intend to insert advertisements this week offering rooms to let, and then the crowds will come."

He led Millie to the left, and they moved down the long corridor together. "You see there was a reason for my neglecting you so. I had to finish up by today. All those visitors thronging into the city, looking for accommodations—and here I am, less than a mile away from Jackson Park, with rooms by the dozen. There's a fortune in it—a fortune!"

"But how can you manage all that and the pharmacy too?"

"Competent help," Gordon said. "In the shop and in the office." He nodded. "You forget, I've the mail-order business to consider. Plus my own private practice as a physician. It's all a matter of proper organization."

Millie noted that the paneled doors they passed were all alike, distinguished only by metal numerals affixed to their upper frames. Gordon halted before one near the end of the hall; its number was 17. His key slid into the lock, the door swung open and he beckoned her forward into the room beyond.

Only it wasn't a room. Millie found herself standing at the foot of another staircase just beyond the doorway.

"Organization," Gordon said, smiling at her as he adjusted the illuminating jet on the inside wall. "A private entrance so that I can come and go without disturbing the tenants."

Millie's eyes traveled the stairway. "But where does this lead to?"

"I'll show you." Gordon moved past her up the stairs, and she followed. There was an odor of fresh paint, of plaster; the stairwell walls seemed scarcely dry to the touch. Millie glanced up to find her husband standing on the topmost stair before yet another door, which opened to his touch. He stood aside, gesturing her forward with a smile of welcome.

"Here we are."

There was no landing here at the head of the stairs; Millie passed directly through the doorway and into a room flaming with light.

The rug was rich and turkey red, setting off the baroquely carved and colorfully cushioned furniture, the scrolled marble mantel of the fireplace, the gilded frames of the oil paintings ornamenting the walls. In the corner was an Estey parlor organ in gleaming solid oak.

Gordon moved up to Millie, enjoying her surprise. "You do like it, then?" he murmured. "I hoped you'd approve."

"Of course . . ." Her smile wavered. "But all this must have cost a fortune."

"I told you I intended to make a fortune. Don't you worry on that account now." He led her across the room to a doorway beyond. "Let me show you the rest."

Again he stood aside, allowing her to precede him across the threshold. There was only a single dim light in the chamber beyond, but that was sufficient; enough to outline the opulence of the cushion-strewn canopy bed dominating the center of the room and to reflect Millie's image in the huge wall mirror beyond.

Staring into the mirror, she saw Gordon smiling beside her.

"Well, my dear, what do you think?"

"It's like a palace!"

"A castle," he said. "A man's home is his castle, you know."

His hand was on her arm; she tingled to the touch. Now was the moment, she told herself. The moment to pull free, face him squarely, confront him with everything remembered and resented during the long months of separation; the excuses, the evasions, the extravagances, her need and his neglect.

But when she faced him she could see his eyes, and she could feel them, feel them even more strongly than his caressing fingers still stealing across her arm. She had always felt them, from the very beginning, felt their stare that was so soft and yet so deep, like the soft, deep voice.

"And what is a castle without a princess?" the voice said.

The voice said and the hands caressed, and Millie could see her own tiny reflection in the pupils of his eyes.

"I've missed you so, my dearest," he said. She was so tiny and his eyes were so enormous and the bed was so soft and deep and now everything was so . . . just so. There was the window on the other wall, and beyond it the glow and glitter of the Fairgrounds against the distant darkness.

Only afterward, when she was lying relaxed in his arms, did the momentary misgivings emerge.

"Happy?" he whispered.

"Oh, yes."

"Then why the frown?" He'd noticed that; he always seemed to sense her mood.

"I'm still thinking . . . all this expense . . ."

The eyes above her twinkled. "A man's entitled to spend a little money on his honeymoon. Even his second honeymoon." The eyes sobered. "Please now, dear heart. Let's not spoil it."

Millie didn't answer. She was remembering that other time, the first honeymoon, and how it had almost been spoiled when she learned of her husband's business activities back East. Of course the money he'd earned had helped pay his way through medical school, but the idea of selling paupers' bodies to anatomy classes always disturbed her.

Gordon had been patient and understanding. When he saw that she was upset, he took care to explain; the practice was not only legitimate but necessary, medical students had to be supplied with specimens in the interest of science. In time Millie came to realize that what really agitated her was her own morbid fear of death, of being buried away underground.

When she explained this to Gordon he understood immediately, and took steps to reassure her that all this was long since over and done with; he was a practicing physician now, and his life was dedicated to the living, not the dead. But he was right; the matter had almost ruined their honeymoon then, and if he knew what she was thinking at this very moment . . .

"You mustn't trouble yourself," he murmured gently. "There's no question of going back to that again."

Millie glanced up at him, then quickly sought to conceal her surprise under lowered lids. He *did* know what was bothering her.

"Listen to me, darling. I have the pharmacy now. The Elixir alone will soon be paying for all expenses. And once the rent from lodgings starts rolling in, we'll make a mint. It's a capital arrangement; you just wait and see how well it goes!"

His enthusiasm was infectious; Millie's misgivings melted as he spoke, and his final words dissolved them once and for all.

"No more of that," he said. "I give you my promise." He bent forward until his lips touched hers. "It's getting late," he murmured. "Time to go to sleep. You must be very tired."

Millie nodded. Yes, she *was* tired. Tired and relieved. It was good to be back with him, so very good to relax, to rest beside him once more in their very own bed.

He lowered her head against the pile of silken pillows and she sank into their softness, into the softness of sleep itself as he held her close, close and safe and warm in his arms.

As the fireworks burst and flared over the distant Fair, Millie stirred but did not waken. Nor did she awake when her husband, smiling in the darkness, groped gently under his own pillow to bring forth the bottle and the cloth with which he saturated its contents. The reek of chloroform filled the room. And then her nostrils, her throat, her lungs, as he pressed the rag against her face.

She struggled then, but the weight of his body pressed her down; there was no strength in her movements, only the strength of his hands, the strength of the sticky-sweet smell that sent her sinking into the final slumber.

It was later, much later, when Dr. G. Gordon Gregg emerged from an inconspicuous side doorway leading out onto Wallace Avenue three stories below. For a moment he stood there, scanning the shadows for a stir of movement, finding none. In the distance he heard the rumble of a midnight train on the elevated railroad, but the street before him was silent.

Satisfied, he took a firmer grip on his burlap burden and carried it over to the curb where the rented hansom waited, the horse still standing patiently at the hitching post. The drive across town was a lengthy one, but nothing disturbed his progress until the clop of hooves halted before the house in Ravenswood.

Once again he waited, peering up and down the thoroughfare until satisfied it was quite deserted. Only then did he tether the horse around at the alley behind; then he shouldered his sack and carried it to the back entrance. His key was ready, and the house was ready too.

Into the bedroom now. Pull off the coverlets in the dark, open the mouth of the sack, arrange its charred contents on the bed. Then dump out the glass at the bottom, the glass and the bottle. Remove the cork, sprinkle the whiskey over the sheets. Alcohol burns as well as kerosene, and if you place an empty bottle and glass on the bedside table, its presence is self-explanatory and excites no suspicion.

There would be kerosene too, of course, from the lamp, but that too was self-explanatory. The lamp is lighted—thus. It accidentally overturns—so. And the blaze begins.

He waited just long enough to make sure, then hurried out into the alley, locking the door behind him.

It took presence and restraint not to whip the horse; no one must hear him clatter away at this hour of the night. But the effort told, and his hands were wet on the reins as the hansom moved into the street.

Only when he was well on his way again could he relax and permit himself to smile, thinking of Millie. At least he'd respected her wishes in the matter. She didn't want to be buried underground.

2

THEY CAME from everywhere this spring and summer of 1893, thronging to the Fair. They came on foot, in carriages and hacks, in horsecars and cable cars and the new electric cars of the elevated railway. They arrived by trainloads at the Transportation Center and by boatloads at the pier.

All the world went to the World's Fair. Pulses quickened at the sight of the White City with its miles of palaces rising in domes and cupolas over the vast central lagoon. Necks craned at the immensity of the Building of Manufacturing and Liberal Arts, its forty acres of floor space sprawling across a site double the size of the Great Pyramid. Ears were deafened by the dynamo din of the Electrical Building and Machinery Hall by day, and eyes were dazzled by night as the structures shimmered in the light of ten thousand incandescent lamps. Bodies jostled in the four great galleries of the Art Palace, the halls of the agricultural displays, mining and fishery, the Horticultural Building. By the millions, weary feet plodded through the Government Building, the exhibitions of forty states and a score of foreign nations.

Crowds gaped at replicas of the *Niña, Pinta* and *Santa Maria* riding serenely at anchor. Families picknicked on the Wooded Island while their children eyed the Indian School, the Egyptian Obelisk, the Logger's Camp and Hagenback's Animal Show or watched the daily parades and processions. And by night, courting couples clung together in the cars of the great Ferris Wheel, soaring two hundred and sixty-five giddy feet into the sky to blink down at the whole wide wonderworld below.

Jim Frazer came to the Fair by day. He came alone, almost stealthily, that warm afternoon late in June. His boss at the insurance agency had given him an errand on the South Side, and if he knew he was playing hookey . . .

But what Mr. Follansbee didn't know wouldn't hurt him. Any more than it would hurt Jim to take advantage of this opportunity to visit a great educational exhibition.

To the west of the Women's Building was a long narrow strip extending past the railroad tracks—a finger of land which, some people thought, stuck out like a sore thumb. Its official designation was the Midway Plaisance, but all Chicago knew it merely as the Midway. And if a fellow was in search of culture and had only an hour to spare, not long enough to see everything at the whole Fair here, he could still come through the entrance at Cottage Grove Avenue and get a quick education just on the Midway itself.

Maybe he couldn't learn so much about lighthouses and heliographs and sewage-cleansing works, but it was nice to see the captive balloon straining against the sky across the way from the Dahomey Village, to sip a glass of wine at the French Village or down a seidel at the Vienna Café while the military band played "Daisy Bell." There were a Chinese Tea House, a Japanese Bazaar, a Dutch Settlement—good beer there, too—a Persian Concession, even a model of St. Peter's in Rome. To say nothing of a World's Congress of Beauty which made a man's throat feel dry, so that it was only natural to stop by at the German Village for the best beer of all. And if you didn't have time for the Ice Railway or the Panorama of Bernese Alps, there was always the Moorish Palace.

Jim had heard there was a Chamber of Horrors inside, but somehow he wasn't exactly in the mood for visiting dungeons on a fine day like this with the band playing "The Man Who Broke the Bank at Monte Carlo." And all the fine folks crowding into the concession just across the way. No, it wasn't the Lecture Hall of the Science of Animal Locomotion they were interested in: after all, doesn't everybody know how a horse trots? But there was another big walled-off display directly behind it.

A Street in Cairo, that was the name. And that was the place they were headed for, the place where the drums were pounding and the music was wailing.

The good ladies of Chicago had been most upset about the Street in Cairo, and Mr. Follansbee would surely throw a conniption fit if he saw his trusted employee join the throng at the entrance. Only Mr. Follansbee wasn't here to see, and even if he were, the chance was unlikely that he'd spot Jim in the mob. He paid and he pushed, pressing forward past the *souks* and the cluster of caftaned Arabs on the cobblestones. To his surprise, he *was* on a street in Cairo, dodging donkeys, rounding a corner to come eye to eye with a camel—which spat at him and missed. There were beggars and peddlers of brassware and a snake charmer squatting beside a basket and tootling away on a horn at a cobra. The serpent uncoiled, rising rhythmically over the rim of the basket to form a swaying question mark.

Strange sights, strange sounds and even stranger smells. But the crowd was moving along, and Jim moved with it, into the alcove, the annex, the apex of the exhibition.

"Strictly for your edification and education, gentlemen," said the suave, smiling barker on the raised platform. And like all the other gentlemen, Jim peered across the footlights as the barker bowed off, the robed musician in the fez raised his flute and the music began.

Little Egypt danced. She was no raving beauty; you'd never mistake this overpainted swarthy specimen for Lillian Russell. But her feet were bare, her legs flashing beneath the filmy skirt were bare—and quite obviously female human legs: not limbs or unmentionables, but the genuine article, complete with ankles and even knees. Her arms were bare too, as she discarded her veil, and so were her shoulders and her bosom beneath the metal breastplates.

Heat rose from the packed crowd before the platform. Jim glanced up for a moment, seeking a breath of air, and as he did so he scanned the faces of his fellow spectators. Here were young hayseeds dressed in go-to-meeting best, sprouting the old-fashioned chin whiskers that betrayed their rural origins as surely as did the red necks chafed by the unaccustomed confinement in celluloid collars. Here were sports in checked vests, their bowlers pushed back on perspiring foreheads. And here were the solid citizens, men of substance—substance carefully tucked into sensible woolen suitings. Men of muttonchops and graying sideburns; men wearing gold watch chains and diamond stickpins and stern, disapproving looks as they squinted through their spectacles at an exhibition that in no way resembled the waltzes and lancers of the fashionable cotillions they attended with their buxom and befrilled wives. But there were no wives here, and they were free to stare and even smile.

Jim shook his head. Too hot in here, too crowded. Suddenly he wondered why he was standing here in this motley mob. *Hutchi-kutchi*—was that what they called it? But it was just a belly dance. A belly dance for a bunch of yokels ashamed to even use the word "belly" in front of their womenfolk.

He turned away, elbowing toward the rear of the enclosure. As he did so he realized that he was ashamed, too. Not at what he'd seen, but at his motives for seeing it. No use pretending he was any better than the rest; he'd come to join this grinning, gaping group for the same reason, and like the others he was grateful there were no ladies present. If Crystal ever found out he'd come here, he'd feel like a damned fool.

Well, at least that was something to be grateful for. Thank God *she'd* never know. Jim plowed quickly in the direction of the exit. Men grumbled, grunted and moved aside, eyes intent on the platform. To Jim it seemed as though half the male population of Chicago choked this crowded cubicle with their brawny bulk.

And then, just as he reached the doorway, his body bumped against softer, yielding flesh. Glancing up quickly, he found himself face to face with a female. She wore a veil lowered discreetly from her hat to cover her features, but it did not disguise her obvious femininity.

Embarrassed, Jim found himself automatically tipping his hat and murmuring: "Excuse me, ma'am."

As he stepped aside he heard the giggle, and then the voice from beneath the veil.

"That's all right, Jim."

He turned, startled, as the veil swept up and he stared into the familiar face.

"Oh no . . ." he murmured.

"Oh yes," said Crystal.

3

OUTSIDE THE ENTRANCE the air was fresh, and Jim gulped it gratefully. Then he turned to the girl he had dragged through the doorway and gulped again.

He searched the face of his fiancée, but as always when seeking a clue, he found only contradiction. The eyes were all doelike demurity, so curiously in contrast to the tilt of her snub nose; the melting mouth held a promise quickly canceled by the stubborn chin beneath. Now she was smiling up at him gravely, and what was *that* supposed to mean?

"Crystal—you followed me—"

"Don't give yourself airs. This is business."

"Business?"

She nodded. "With all those do-gooders up in arms over Little Egypt, I thought it would be nice to get a story on her from the woman's angle."

"But women aren't supposed to see such things!"

"What things? Women know all about the female body. It's you men who are the ignorant ones."

Jim felt himself reddening.

"I wish you wouldn't talk that way. It's not becoming in a lady."

"I'm not a lady. I'm a reporter; that's why I'm here." Crystal eyed him directly. "What's your excuse?"

"Well, I just happened to be in the neighborhood and I thought—" Jim hesitated as Crystal giggled again.

"Come off it! Why don't you tell the truth and admit you were curious, just like all the rest?" She shook her head. "Sometimes I wonder what on earth I see in you."

But she squeezed his arm, and as they turned to move down the Midway she was smiling.

"You haven't said what you thought of the performance."

Jim shook his head cautiously. "It wasn't exactly what I expected . . ."

"Were you hoping she'd be naked?" She peered at him inquiringly. "Go ahead, tell me. I might be able to quote you in my article."

"You're not really going to write a story about this?"

"Of course I will! Whether or not they'll print it is another matter." Crystal frowned. "Sometimes I think my editor is more of an old lady than the biddies who run the Society Pages."

Jim sighed. "Well, he hired you. And there aren't very many who'd have the nerve to employ a female reporter."

"Why not? Half the world is female. Women buy papers just as men do. And we're just as capable at finding news as we are at reading it. What about Nellie Bly, going around the world in eighty days?"

"It wasn't eighty days. And I hope you don't think you're like that Bly woman."

Crystal nodded quickly. "I'm not going to smoke cigars, if that's what you mean."

"Glad to hear it."

"I tried to, once, and got deathly ill."

"Serves you right."

Crystal was thoughtful. "Of course it was a very *cheap* cigar. Perhaps if I had a good one . . ."

Jim found himself grinning. "Sorry, I'm fresh out."

"Then maybe I'll let you buy me a parfait instead. They say there's a lovely sidewalk café here, just like the ones in Paris."

"Some other time." Jim tugged at his watch chain, lifted the watch from its pocket, snapped the case open to inspect the face. "I have a business appointment."

"But it's such a beautiful day . . ."

"Look, I've got an idea. Why don't you come with me? It's just a few blocks away, and I won't be long. Then we can come back here for dinner."

Crystal smiled. "Let's go."

Jim guided her toward the exit, and they emerged on the street to confront a cluster of cabbies congregating before a row of hansoms and hacks for hire.

Jim glanced over at the girl. "If you don't mind, I thought we'd walk over. It isn't far."

"Of course." Crystal moved with him to the corner crossing. "But you still haven't told me where we're going."

"That's right, I haven't." Jim gripped her arm as they crossed the street and headed west. "I'm taking you to a castle."

4

THE PHARMACY was busy that afternoon.

As Crystal entered she lowered her veil discreetly, but Jim's vision was unobstructed. Most of the customers, he observed, were women, and the majority of them were purchasing proprietary medicines from the well-stocked shelves. Two young clerks in shirt sleeves stood behind the front counter, waiting on trade and ringing up sales on the cash register. Its constant clang punctuated the proceedings with a note of prosperity.

At the far end of the counter, an older man in a white jacket pored over a prescription ledger. Jim led Crystal there, then stood patiently until he was noticed.

"Good afternoon. Can I help you?"

"Mr. Gregg?"

The older man shook his head. "I'm Mr. Hickey." He peered at Jim over rimless spectacles. "Was it a prescription matter?"

"No, I called him this morning. We have an appointment."

"I'll see if I can locate him." The eyes behind the lenses were narrowed in wary appraisal. "Who should I say—?"

"Tell him Jim Frazer wants to see him."

"Wait here, please."

The man moved along the counter and disappeared through the dispensary doorway beyond.

Jim glanced at Crystal. "Quite a place, isn't it?"

Crystal groaned beneath her veil. "I'm not sure I understand. Who'd think of putting a drugstore in a castle—a patent-medicine king?"

"I gather that's what he is, in a way." Jim shrugged. "Actually, it's a long story—" He broke off abruptly as Hickey emerged from the doorway at the end of the counter, followed by a tall man wearing a white suit.

White suit and matching linen—and a sudden smile, displaying white teeth in a pale white face. All of which made the black hair and moustache that more startling in contrast; or was the real contrast in the dark depths of the eyes? But the eyes were smiling too. They glanced casually at Crystal, then focused on Jim with courteous concern.

"I'm Gordon Gregg. Sorry to have kept you waiting like this. If you'll be good enough to come with me to my office, Mr. Frazer . . ."

Jim glanced at Crystal. "Will you excuse me?"

For a moment there was no answer. She seemed to be

staring at Gregg from behind her veil. Then she nodded. "Certainly."

But she was still staring as Jim turned away and followed Gregg behind the counter to the doorway at the rear of the shop.

"This way."

Jim moved with Gregg through the prescription dispensary to another door on the right. Gregg pushed it open, stood aside, gestured at Jim to precede him. "Here we are."

They were in a handsomely furnished business office with a rolltop desk dominating the far wall, built-in bookshelves on both sides and a second desk near a door at one side. On top of the desk was a new typewriting machine, and behind it sat an operator.

Jim caught a glimpse of ash-blond hair and gray eyes as the secretary rose in response to Gregg's murmur. "You can go now, Alice. I'll finish the dictation upstairs."

The girl smiled, gathered up a notebook and a pencil from the desktop, then moved to disappear through the side door.

Gregg crossed to the desk, seated himself and indicated a chair at one side.

"Sit down, Mr. Frazer; make yourself at home."

Jim complied, glancing at the imposing array of framed diplomas and certificates on the wall beside the telephone and the medical texts that filled the bookshelves. He'd been in plenty of doctors' offices, but seldom one as impressive; Gregg must have had at least half a dozen degrees.

"Can I offer you some refreshment?"

"No, thank you."

"Not during business hours, eh?" Gregg nodded approvingly. "Very sensible policy. I happen to be a teetotaler myself. Not a question of moral principle, you understand—just common sense. In my profession one sees too many horrible examples of the consequences of overindulgence." Gregg's smile faded. "My late wife—"

Jim glanced up quickly as the older man shrugged.

"You might as well know the truth," Gregg said. "I'm sure you must have wondered how it happened."

Jim nodded. He had wondered, and he wasn't the only one. The fire department puzzled over the blaze that had destroyed Gregg's home in Ravenswood, leveling it to ashes in the night. The medical examiners who identified Millicent Gregg's body through bridgework and jewelry couldn't account for why she hadn't made her escape from the conflagration. And of course Mr. Follansbee wondered most of all. Before paying out on a life-insurance policy under such circumstances, it's reasonable to examine the facts.

But the facts were simple. The fire marshal found no evidence of arson; apparently a night lamp had fallen in the bedroom. The coroner discovered no signs of violence, no marks or bruises on the body—or what remained of it; Millicent Gregg had died in her own bed, where the lamp had fallen. So Mr. Follansbee finally found himself facing the most disagreeable fact of all: the death was accidental, and the company must pay.

"Ironic, isn't it?" Gregg was saying. "Alcoholism is a disease—that, sir, happens to be my professional opinion. And as a medical man, it's my duty to deal with disease in any form. But here was such a case in my own home, under my very eyes, and I didn't recognize it until too late. Far too late!"

"You didn't know?"

"That she drank?" Gregg shrugged again. "We were accustomed to take wine at dinner, yes. And there was the occasional social glass at a party. But I wasn't aware of the secret addiction, the bottles of cordials concealed and consumed, the solitary tippling when I was away." He sighed. "Unfortunately, during the past six months I was away all too frequently. While supervising the construction of this building, I left her alone for long periods of time. When, by chance, I learned how she passed her days, how she literally drank herself into a stupor at night as an antidote to solitude—"

"I understand," Jim murmured.

"She promised to stop," Gregg said. "And I know she meant to keep her word, poor darling. But I should have realized the craving was out of hand." He gestured quickly. "Here, with every remedy known to modern science at my command, I failed to fulfill my duty. Perhaps I didn't want to accept the bitter truth. It might have meant sending her away for a cure, and with the building finally completed, I expected we'd be together again. I was a fool, Mr. Frazer. Worse than a fool." He stared at Jim. "I murdered her."

"Murdered?"

"Yes. I'm responsible for her death. It was my willful blindness that killed her." Gregg broke off, turned away.

"But it wasn't your fault," Jim said. "You mustn't feel that way."

"That's what I try to tell myself. But how can I be sure? After the fire, during the inquest and the investigation, I kept silent. I felt these facts would shame my wife's memory, that I'd be placing blame on the dead. But now I've come to realize the blame is on the living, and the real shame is my own." Gregg shook his head. "My only consolation is the knowledge that Millicent has gone to her final rest. As for me, I shall never find peace."

Silently, Jim reached for his wallet, removed the insurance check, placed it on the desk. Gregg didn't look at it.

"If you'll be good enough to sign this receipt." Jim unfolded the form and laid it before Gregg. *Received from Dearborn Mutual Life Assurance Co., the sum of ten thousand dollars, payment in full for . . .*

Gregg didn't look at the wording of the receipt either; he merely turned and took Jim's proffered pen, signing quickly and handing back the pen and paper without a change of expression.

"I'm sorry," he said. "It's just that I had to speak. And you are entitled to know the truth."

"I understand." Jim rose, pocketing the receipt. It wasn't the first time he'd confronted grief and remorse; such reactions were commonplace in transactions of this sort, and he'd learned to make the expected responses. The phrases came automatically from his lips. "I know how you must feel, but you mustn't reproach yourself. Time is a great healer."

Gregg summoned the wan ghost of a smile. "How often I've used those very words to comfort the bereaved. But I suppose you're right. And there's another phrase I try to remember: Physician, heal thyself."

A buzzer sounded. Gregg stood up and crossed to a speaking-tube unit mounted on the wall beside the safe in the corner.

"Yes, Hickey, what is it?" He listened, frowning. "Tell Mr. O'Leary I'll be with him in a moment."

He glanced at Jim. "Will you excuse me now? I have some business to attend to."

"Of course." Jim moved to the door. "You needn't bother to show me out. I know the way."

Gregg gave him a grateful nod. "Thank you, Mr. Frazer. Thank you for everything."

Jim left, closing the door behind him. Walking back down the hall toward the pharmacy, he breathed a sigh of relief. At least that was over with. He always hated such errands; no matter how often he performed them, it was still embarrassing to deal with the emotional outbursts of the survivors. And Gregg, despite his efforts to maintain a professional aplomb, was deeply shaken.

Well, perhaps time would heal that wound. Jim hoped so, for Gregg's sake, poor devil.

5

THE SIDEWALK CAFÉ may not have been exactly like the ones in Paris, but the food was good, the evening breeze from the lake was cool and the view of the White City was spectacular.

Crystal put down her demitasse and stared off at the vista beyond the Midway where the domes of the Fair loomed against the night. Somewhere behind the blare of calliopes and the clatter of the passing crowd, she heard a hurdy-gurdy playing.

Jim reached across the table and put his hand over hers. "A penny for your thoughts."

Crystal shook her head and smiled up at him. "They're not worth it."

"Look, I just paid out a big claim this afternoon to a total stranger. I can afford to be a little extravagant with you."

"How big a claim? You never told me how much."

"That's right, I didn't. Mr. Follansbee doesn't like for anyone to discuss company transactions. But if you must know, the amount was ten thousand."

"That's a lot of money."

Jim nodded. "He had it coming."

Crystal's smile disappeared, but her eyes were still intent on Jim's face. "You're sure of that?"

"Of course. I told you we investigated. Accidental death, that's double indemnity. You can bet old Follansbee doesn't pay off in such cases unless he's absolutely certain."

"And just what was it that convinced him?"

"The medical report. The fire marshal's statement." Jim gestured at her. "Since when did you get so interested in the insurance business?"

"It's not the business that interests me."

"What is it, then, the circumstances? I told you what Gregg said today. His wife had been drinking heavily. She must have been intoxicated, perhaps even unconscious when the blaze started." Jim took Crystal's hand again, squeezing it quickly. "Promise me you won't turn into an alcoholic after we're married."

"Don't be ridiculous."

"Which reminds me." Jim grinned, but his eyes were earnest. "When are you going to stop being ridiculous and set the date?"

"Just as soon as you change those old-fashioned notions of yours about working wives."

"But I don't want you spending your time in a newspaper office. A woman's place is in the home."

"Mrs. Gregg was in her home, and look what happened to her."

"Please, it's nothing to joke about."

Crystal nodded. It wasn't funny, of course: a helpless woman, trapped in flames, burning to death.

"No sense being morbid," Jim said. "Let's forget about Mrs. Gregg. It's our future I'm interested in."

"Yes." Crystal nodded again. Maybe she was being morbid. Surely Mrs. Gregg meant nothing to her. Jim was right; it was their future that was important. Why hadn't she set a date for the wedding; why did she find herself reluctant to commit herself now? After all, she wanted to marry Jim. He'd make a good husband, a good father, even though he'd probably never be what they called a good provider. If he wanted to, he could work for Mr. Follansbee all his life, and that was undoubtedly his intention. He wasn't the sort to have ambitions about taking over the agency or starting one on his own.

"You're not listening to me," Jim murmured.

Crystal shook her head in automatic denial, but her thoughts were far away. Jim wasn't the only man in the world. Suppose she were to marry someone else? Not one of the reporters she knew at work; they were clods for the most part, notoriously unreliable. But there were others—men of action and accomplishment, men who weren't afraid to gamble for high stakes in the game of life. Men like Gordon Gregg, for example.

How old would he be? Probably still in his thirties, but already an established physician and a successful businessman. Give him another ten years and there was no telling how high he'd soar. He wasn't a plodder, a stick-in-the-mud like Jim.

But what was she doing, comparing Gordon Gregg with her fiancé? It was absurd, the way he'd popped into her mind. After all, she'd never even been introduced to the man, scarcely set eyes on him for a moment. And he hadn't really impressed her—his white suit was somehow as theatrical a conceit as that architectural monstrosity he'd built. But he had built it; he was the kind who turned his dreams to realities. He had the eyes of a dreamer; there was an elusive quality in his glance, something attractive and yet—

"Crystal!"

Jim's voice. The voice of reason. "What's got into you? Don't tell me you're still thinking about this afternoon?"

Crystal hesitated, summoning a smile. Jim might be a plodder, but he wasn't a fool. She might as well admit the truth. "Yes. Your Mr. Gregg."

"What about him?"

"I don't know." And she didn't know, but there must be some reason why this stranger had made such a troubling impression. "Jim—how long did you say it's been since Gregg's wife passed away?"

"She died on the first of May. The night the Fair opened."

"But that's only a little over six weeks ago."

"I know." Jim shook his head. "No wonder he's still so upset. Poor chap, he almost broke down while we were talking about it."

"He really loved her, then?"

"Of course he did. Just the way I love you." Jim's hand found hers again and gripped it firmly. "Now, let's not have any more evasions, young lady. I want a straight answer this time. When are you going to marry me?"

A straight answer. That was what she wanted, too—a straight answer about Gregg. Funny how he kept coming back into her mind. *His wife had died on the night the Fair opened . . .*

"When the Fair closes," Crystal said. "We'll get married then."

"You really mean it?"

"Yes."

Jim leaned across the table and kissed her. She sensed his excitement, his exultation, and yet her thoughts were still far away.

"I'll buy the ring tomorrow," Jim said, getting up from the table and helping her to rise.

They walked slowly toward the glittering Ferris Wheel. Jim led her toward it.

"Come on, let's take a ride!"

"All right." It was a diversion. Anything would help to distract her mind from coming back to—what? But even high in the air, Crystal found that her thoughts kept returning to Mr. Gregg, round and round in the same dizzying circle as the swaying car.

"It's in that place near Dearborn and Wabash downtown," Jim was saying. "I've had my eye on it for weeks. Wait until you see it."

He was talking about the ring, of course. The engagement ring formed a circle too. Like a wedding ring. You wore it all your life, till death did you part. And then you wore something else. Something else that was round and black.

As she stared out over the Fairgrounds, the answer came to her. The lights were white, white and bright—like the suit Gregg had worn this afternoon. Poor bereaved Mr. Gregg had been wearing a white suit.

But he hadn't been wearing a mourning band.

6

G. GORDON GREGG had never been busier, and that, he told himself, was his salvation. Or perhaps he wasn't using the right word. Salvation is of no concern to anyone but the dead, and he was very much alive. Alive, active and alert, that was the ticket.

He seated himself behind his desk after young Frazer departed, and he was still sitting there when Bryan O'Leary arrived. There was no mistaking his coming. First the heavy tread of footsteps lumbering down the hall, then the noxious stench of the cheap stogie that seemed forever fixed between his lips. And finally, looming in the doorway, the fleshy face with its bristled jowls, the small eyes peering out from beneath the brim of the derby perched on the bullet head.

Gregg smiled up at him. "Mr. O'Leary—how good to see you!"

"Is it?" Smoke belched from the cigar. "Is it, now?"

"Of course." Gregg rose, gestured. "Here, do sit down. I was just remarking to myself what a coincidence it was—your coming here. I've been thinking about you."

O'Leary's eyes were wary. "And just what were you thinking? Is it some new dodge you have in mind to keep from paying up?"

Gregg's smile broadened. "You shame me, sir. If you'll recall our last conversation—"

"That I do." There was no smile behind O'Leary's cigar. "I brought in my bill and you put me off."

"Please! I told you I'd be in a position to pay as soon as I came into my inheritance."

O'Leary shook his head. "We don't have any secrets in the construction game, Mr. Gregg. I've been talking to the Dutchman about you."

"Dutchman?"

"Charlie Schultz. He and his boys worked on this building before you called me in to finish up."

"I remember Mr. Schultz."

"And he remembers you." O'Leary frowned grimly. "When he came for his money, you said he'd have to wait until you sold your invention. Later you told him the deal fell through."

"But—"

"What about Mike Rogowsky? He laid the foundation and put up the scaffolding before you fired the Dutchman. You were going to refinance the job with a mortgage loan, but he's still whistling for his money."

"The bank turned me down. It couldn't be helped."

O'Leary's eyebrows rose behind a puff of smoke. "I'm on to your tricks, Mr. Gregg. It's half a dozen crews you've had on this castle of yours, hiring and firing them but paying none. But it won't wash, not with yours truly." O'Leary's voice was rising along with his eyebrows. "I'll not be diddled. And I'll not listen to any more of your fancy gab about inheritances. Money talks, Mr. Gregg, if you catch my meaning, and that's all I want to hear. Money talks!"

"So it does."

Gregg reached into his jacket and drew forth his insurance check, unfolding it and placing it face upward on the table before him. "Is this loud enough for you?"

O'Leary stared down at the check. "Ten thousand . . ." His voice trailed off in a reverent hush, and there was reverence in his gesture as he removed the cigar from between his lips. Then the squinting eyes peered up at Gregg. "Where'd you get this?"

"I told you I had an inheritance coming," Gregg murmured. "The check arrived only a few moments ago. Now do you believe me?"

O'Leary nodded. "Then it's an apology I'm owing you."

"And I owe you your fee."

"You'll be paying me now?" O'Leary smiled quickly, expectantly.

"Shortly."

O'Leary's smile disappeared as swiftly as it had come. "What do you mean?"

"I mean that this check must be deposited in my account. I imagine it will take a few days to clear through the bank—say, by next Monday or Tuesday—before I'm free to draw anything against it."

"You're sure it's good?"

Gregg shrugged. "If you have any doubts, call the insurance company yourself."

O'Leary hesitated. "How soon do I get my money, then?"

Gregg picked up the check. "Let's say Wednesday, just to be on the safe side." He folded the check deliberately, precisely, and O'Leary's eyes followed it as it disappeared once again into Gregg's pocket. "Look, I'll be away from here Wednesday on a business appointment, but I intend to be back again by evening. Why not stop in then? Would eight o'clock be convenient?"

"Eight it is." O'Leary put the cigar back into his mouth, moved to the doorway, then paused to glance over at Gregg once more. "Mind you, none of your tricks, now. I want to see cash on the line. If you're not here when I come by, I'll be paying a little visit to some friends of mine down at City Hall."

"I'll be here." Gregg's smile came easily. "I promise you that."

"Good night to you, then." O'Leary tilted the brim of his derby and disappeared through the doorway.

Gregg sat there listening to the sound of footsteps receding along the hall, the closing of the door beyond. Then he rose, moved to the speaking tube on the wall, buzzed twice and lifted the mouthpiece.

"Hickey?"

The response came from the receiver. "Yes, Mr. Gregg?"

"You can close up shop now."

"I haven't totaled the receipts yet."

"Don't bother. I'll tend to it."

"Thank you, sir."

"Good night. See you in the morning."

"Right you are. Seven o'clock sharp."

Gregg replaced the speaking tube, smiling to himself. Good old Hickey: never a cross word, never a question. He just attended to business from morning till night and ran the store as conscientiously as if it were his very own. Nothing like a faithful employee, and Hickey was a jewel.

Gregg extinguished the gas jet, then moved into the hall. It was quite dark, but the skeleton key in his hand fitted unerringly into the lock at the landing. He ascended the stairs in darkness and hurried down the corridor above. Now the key turned in the door of Room 17. He tiptoed through the doorway, climbing the staircase quickly and quietly, then entered the brightly lit parlor beyond, where his secretary awaited him.

Alice Porter was sitting in an armchair, a wineglass in her hand and a decanter on the table beside her. The ash-blond hair tumbled over her shoulders, and the robe she was wearing afforded a vivid contrast to her office attire.

She frowned up at Gregg, then rose, putting down her empty glass. "What's been keeping you?"

"This." Gregg exhibited the check.

Alice's eyes widened. "You got it. You really got it!"

"I told you I would."

The wide eyes were intent as Gregg folded the check and slipped it back into his pocket. Then they narrowed. "You told me a lot of things . . ."

"And I meant them, every one." Gregg nodded calmly. "Tomorrow I'll deposit this in the private account. Then you can keep your part of the bargain. I want you to go down to Saint Louis next week and sell that property your parents left you."

"But I don't want to sell the house. It's all I own."

"You forget, half of what I have is yours too. From now

on, we share everything." Gregg searched her face. "When you come back with the money, we'll put it with mine in a new account—all of it, under a new name."

"What name?"

"Mrs. G. Gordon Gregg."

Alice's eyes glowed, then clouded with uncertainty. "You're always promising . . ." She shook her head. "I'll believe it when I see it."

"Then look at this."

Gregg drew the little plush-covered box from his vest pocket and snapped up the lid. The diamond sparkled and glittered; he could see its reflection in her pupils as she stared.

"A ring?"

"For our engagement. When you return from your trip, there'll be another. A plain gold band." Gregg smiled, extending the box. "Here; don't you want to wear it?"

He stood there watching as she slipped it on; her fingers were trembling, and her voice was trembling too, as she held her hand up to the light.

"It fits, doesn't it?" he murmured.

"Perfectly. Oh, darling, it's so beautiful . . ."

Gregg smiled. His arms gently circled her waist.

7

On Saturday, Jim Frazer went downtown and bought Crystal's engagement ring. It was priced under a hundred dollars, and the stone was nowhere near the size of the one Gregg had presented to Alice Porter. But neither Jim nor Crystal had seen the other piece of jewelry, and this seemed impressive enough to them both.

On Sunday Crystal wore the ring for the first time, when she and Jim went to the Coliseum. Crystal had press passes for Buffalo Bill's Wild West Show, and they enjoyed the performance. But while Crystal thrilled to the famous Indian attack on the Deadwood Coach, Jim's eyes found more fascination in the sparkle of the diamond on her finger.

Monday Jim reported to Mr. Follansbee regarding his

visit to G. Gordon Gregg. The old man didn't seem exactly overjoyed—it wasn't every day that the Dearborn Mutual Life Assurance Company had to cough up ten thousand simoleons in payment of a claim—but he was satisfied with Jim's account of the transaction. "Be sure you mention it when you're seeing prospects," he said. "Talk it up. Won't hurt to let them know we pay off our claims, no matter how big they are. Here's a list of leads I want you to look into this week. Now get going; we've got to make back that money."

On Tuesday, Crystal's editor, Charlie Hogan, ran her piece on Little Egypt in the morning edition.

Anyone seeing the red-haired newspaperman behind the desk for the first time would argue that he was entirely too youthful to be the city editor of one of Chicago's leading dailies, but Crystal had learned to respect the intelligence behind the twinkling blue eyes, the warm Irish grin. And now his praise meant a great deal to her.

"Looks like we'll make a reporter out of you yet, Crissie," he said. "It's a damned good job."

"Then why didn't you run it the way I wrote it? All that stuff you put in about the Dance of the Seven Veils with six of the veils missing—"

"It sells papers. Stirs up the old ladies and the Sunday-school superintendents. If you can come up with a few more ideas like this, I'll see that you get a five-dollar raise."

"What about a by-line?"

"We'll see. Got anything in mind?"

"Yes. I want to do a series on Little Cheyenne, Custom House Place, Hell's Half Acre."

"Forget it. Every rag in town has already done exposé stuff on the red-light district."

"Yes, by male reporters. But never from the woman's angle. Now do you see why I want a by-line?"

"What's your slant?"

"The Fair. Ever since it opened, those places have been booming. Mayor Harrison and the City Hall crowd promised a wide-open town, and they've kept their word. Thousands of visitors are being fleeced night and day in gambling joints, cribs, parlor houses—"

"What do you know about such things?"

"What everybody in town knows, and doesn't dare talk about. And I can find out more." Crystal nodded firmly. "Give me this assignment and you'll sell papers!"

"Sure we will. To Carter Harrison and the boys at City Hall. Then they'll all be on our necks."

"Just my neck, if it's my by-line."

"But it's such a pretty neck, Crissie. Why do you want to stick it out? A nice young lady like you, engaged and everything—"

"Makes a good story, doesn't it?"

Charlie Hogan grinned. "You've got me there, I guess."

"And have I got a by-line?"

"Maybe. Now go to work."

Crystal floated out of the office. All the rest of that day her head was in the clouds. She didn't tell Jim, of course; she knew what his reaction would be. *A woman's place is in the home, not a parlor house.* There were times when Jim reminded her very much of her father. Daddy had been prim and proper too. Maybe being a minister's daughter had played a part in determining her rebellion against restraint. It wasn't until Daddy died that she'd determined to take up journalism. But she didn't resent her father; he'd been good to her, as Jim was good to her now. It was just that neither of them really understood her. So when she met Jim for dinner she neglected to mention her new assignment, and Tuesday evening passed quietly for them both.

On Wednesday Bryan O'Leary went back to the castle. He wore the same old battered derby, but his cigar was fresh and a good deal more fragrant than the one he'd smoked on his previous visit. No more of those nickel stogies for yours truly; a man who's about to receive a nice, fat fee is entitled to a nice, fat Havana.

Gregg was happy to see him. At least he said he was delighted, and he looked happy enough when he opened the pharmacy door in response to the night buzzer.

"Eight o'clock," he said. "I see that promptness is one of your many virtues."

O'Leary nodded. Gregg seemed to be in fine fettle, and that was a good sign. He was wearing a brand-new outfit—fancy checked suit and a tie with a diamond stickpin—and that was a good sign too. Must have cashed his check all right; no trouble there.

"In we go," Gregg told him.

They moved through the darkened pharmacy, and O'Leary half-expected Gregg to lead him into his office. Instead, he was guided to a hall beyond. They halted before a paneled door. O'Leary watched as his host unlocked the door, opened it, turned up a gas jet in the passageway across the threshold. A narrow staircase slanted upward. Gregg gestured toward the steeply pitched steps.

"Recognize this?"

"That I do. I built it."

"Then you know what it leads to." Gregg started up the stairs.

O'Leary paused behind him. "Why up there?" he asked.

"Because that's where the money is. The other night you

said something about cash on the line." Gregg shrugged. "It's bad business to keep that much lying around in the office, so I'm afraid you'll have to climb for it."

And a long climb it was up those steps—two full flights without a landing. O'Leary remembered his surprise when he'd been told to build the staircase straight through to the third story, bypassing the second floor entirely. At the time he'd wondered why the stairs were needed at all, because another flight ran almost parallel with them on the other side of the wall. But that set ended on the second floor and this one went right to the top.

He was panting by the time he got there and Gregg unlocked the door, and it was a relief to move from the stuffy stairwell into the comfortable room beyond. This was another office he stood in now, smaller than the one downstairs but completely furnished. He glanced at the desk, the wooden filing cabinets, the life-sized anatomy chart on the wall and the big wall safe beside it with a walk-in door.

O'Leary turned to see Gregg closing the door through which they'd entered. From this side it fitted tightly against the wall, and like the wall itself it was covered with striped paper. The stripes hid the outline of the door itself; flush with the wall and without a protruding knob, it was completely invisible.

Gregg seemed amused by his surprise. "Now you know my secret," he said. "I'm a great believer in privacy, particularly when there's money to be protected."

He moved to the desk, opened the drawer below it and turned, holding a bottle of whiskey in his hand. "I trust you're not averse to a slight libation?"

O'Leary shook his head. "You were saying about the money—"

"Of course." Gregg put the bottle down on the desk next

to a water carafe and glasses. "First things first, eh?"

He crossed to the far wall. O'Leary watched, expecting him to go to the safe, but instead he halted in front of the anatomy chart. His fingers snapped against the base, and the gaudy red-and-blue-veined figure disappeared, rolling upward to reveal the bare plaster behind. Set in the wall was a recessed niche, and set in the niche was an ordinary tin box. Gregg pulled it out and opened the lid. His hand dipped inside and emerged, clutching a bundle of greenbacks encircled by a plain rubber band. He turned and tossed the wad of currency to O'Leary.

"Here you are," he said. "You'll want to count it, I suppose."

O'Leary nodded. As he sank into the chair beside the desk, his stubby fingers were already riffling through the sheaf of banknotes.

Gregg moved around the desk to take his seat behind it. "Two thousand," he murmured. "Is that correct?"

O'Leary nodded again. "Right you are."

"Twenty-one hundred, to be exact," Gregg said.

O'Leary's beetle brows crawled into a frown. The doctor had caught him out; might as well admit it, damn him. "By golly, I must have miscounted." Reluctantly he started to peel the topmost hundred-dollar bill from the sheaf, but Gregg halted his movement with a casual gesture.

"Don't trouble yourself. It's worth the extra hundred to prove a theory."

"And just what might that theory be?"

"That you're a dirty, thieving scoundrel." Gregg chuckled. "And a man after my own heart."

Bryan O'Leary blinked.

"Don't play the innocent with me," Gregg was saying. "I knew you for a rascal the moment I set eyes on you. No doubt your mother was the Mrs. O'Leary whose cow kicked over the lantern to start the Chicago Fire."

He chuckled again, and O'Leary felt his own face relax into a smile. "Now put your money away," Gregg commanded. "And let's have that drink."

Queer it was how you could misjudge a man. All along he'd thought Gregg was just another one of your stuffed shirts. Sharp in his dealings, of course, and someone to bear watching, but always the perfect gentleman. Yet here he was, grinning like a Cheshire cat and pouring a stiff dollop of good bonded rye from the bottle into a glass.

O'Leary rolled the bills, tightened the rubber band around them and thrust the bundle into his coat pocket. He reached for the glass Gregg extended to him, then hesitated.

"Aren't you joining me?"

"Certainly." Gregg was filling his own glass from the water carafe.

"You'll not be drinking water?" O'Leary said.

Gregg shook his head. "Something far better than water. Better than whiskey, too."

"And what could that be?"

"My own invention." Gregg lifted his glass to the light, inspecting its contents critically. "This, sir, is Electric Elixir."

O'Leary squinted. "Looks like water to me."

"Indeed. But not your ordinary *aqua pura.* This water has been magnetized, fortified by the passage of a galvanic current through its contents—energizing and enriching it with the vital essence of life itself." Gregg halted, nodding. "Perhaps you'd prefer to join me in a glass?"

O'Leary scowled. "It's a drink I'm wanting, not a purge!"

Gregg laughed. "I thought as much. You're a man who knows his own mind."

"And yours." O'Leary winked at his host. "Just between the two of us, now, I'm of the opinion this concoction is straight out of Lake Michigan. Any fool knows that passing current through water will electrocute you."

Gregg laughed again. "You're wrong," he said. "That's precisely what any fool doesn't know. Which is why I'm doing a land-office business drawing this straight from the tap and selling it across the counter at ten cents a drink."

"You're a bit of a rascal yourself, I'm thinking," said O'Leary.

Gregg shrugged. "You know the old saying: it takes one to know one." He lifted his glass.

"I'll drink to that," said Bryan O'Leary.

And he did.

Ten seconds later he was writhing on the floor. Thirty seconds and he was rigid, so rigid that he couldn't lift a finger when Gregg bent over him and lifted the roll of bills from his pocket.

A minute more and he was not only rigid but numb. He was vaguely aware of being dragged across the floor toward the open doorway of a small bathroom beyond. His glazed eyes scarcely distinguished Gregg's leg as the doctor kicked a small rug aside, disclosing a trapdoor in the floor. Bending forward, Gregg opened the door, then pushed O'Leary's body forward.

As O'Leary rolled to the edge of the opening, he heard Gregg's voice, faint and faraway. He wasn't sure what Gregg was saying, but it sounded like "Paid in full."

O'Leary's final glimpse was of the hole in the floor as he toppled forward. It was deep, dark, yawning. *Why, it's like a mouth,* he thought.

Then it swallowed him.

8

LOVE at first sight. It happened in books, it happened in popular songs, but Genevieve never quite believed it ever happened in real life. And she certainly never thought it could happen to her.

In the beginning, she wasn't even aware of what was going on. All she knew was that she felt very flustered and ill at ease, standing there in his office and seeing those important-looking diplomas and things on the wall. It was all she could do to answer his questions.

He sat behind his desk looking at the card they'd given her at Miss Garland's College of Business.

"So you're the young lady who's interested in a position here," he said. "Can you typewrite?"

"Yes."

"Have you ever worked as a secretary before, Miss—?"

"Bolton." Her voice was husky, and she swallowed quickly. "Genevieve Bolton."

He glanced up quickly. Maybe that was when it really happened, when she saw his eyes. Those dark, warm, wonderful eyes. But if so, she still didn't realize any such thing at the time; all she knew was that her knees were going weak.

"Please sit down, Miss Bolton," he said. "You mustn't be nervous."

It was a relief to sink down into the chair beside the desk, and he seemed to understand just how she felt.

"Here, this may help."

He poured something from a carafe into a crystal glass, holding it up for her inspection.

"Do you see what I have for you?"

Genevieve nodded, puzzled by his question. "A glass of water."

"Take a good look."

Genevieve gazed at the glass as he twirled it between his fingers so that the crystal facets sparkled beneath the bright light.

"See how it shines," he said.

The contents of the glass began to shimmer before her eyes, and she wanted to blink, but his voice told her to look until she could perceive the purity and the power of electromagnetic energy. She had never heard of the Electric Elixir before, but he was explaining it to her now, telling her of the wonderful soothing and healing effects of natural electrical forces.

And that, perhaps, is when it did happen to her, when he gave her the glass and his hand accidentally touched hers, so that she felt the tingling. Or did the tingling come when she drank the Elixir and its coolness soothed and spread, just as he had said it would? All she knew was that suddenly there was no more tension, only a vibrant feeling of being alive and alert, so that she could answer questions quite easily. And when he smiled, even his questions were no longer necessary. She found herself telling him everything he wanted to know about her.

Not that there was much to tell. Growing up on a farm just outside Kansas City; going to live in town with Uncle Fred after her folks passed away in the typhoid epidemic; coming here to Chicago to study at business college when Uncle Fred died. How could such dull things possibly interest anyone like Dr. Gregg?

But he *was* interested, and in the days that followed he asked her all sorts of questions about her life. The funny part was, *she* wasn't interested. As far as Genevieve was concerned, her life hadn't really begun until now. The past didn't seem real anymore; all that mattered was Gordon.

Yes, it was Gordon now and not Dr. Gregg. And when had that happened? Try as she might, she couldn't exactly recall.

She remembered accepting the position, moving into the furnished room on the second floor, working with him in his office. But all those things blurred into the background; only Gordon was important: Gordon's eyes smiling at her as he dictated, Gordon's voice soft and melancholy when he spoke of his bereavement, his loneliness.

It was then, perhaps, that she stopped thinking of him as the imposing, important Dr. Gregg and began to glimpse the gentle, troubled man beneath the title and the degrees, the benefactor of humanity who himself was in need of comfort and compassion.

Everything happened so quickly, though that was understandable; after all, even in the first few days they spent so much time together. Genevieve scarcely set eyes on the pharmacy up front or the people who worked there. Her life was in the office with Gordon and then in the apartment above. In the beginning, the idea of dining alone with a man in his private quarters was a trifle disconcerting. But it did make it easier to carry on with the dictation, and there was so much correspondence to attend to. Besides, the apartment itself was such a lovely place, with all those gorgeous furnishings; it was far nicer than the office, where people were always interrupting. Here she and Gordon could be alone, relaxing over luncheon or those dinners he had sent in from the restaurant down the street. Even though she wrote those letters, she didn't really feel she was working at all. It was more as if she and Gordon were sharing a home together.

She fully realized the degree of her feelings the day he excused himself and spent over two hours with Mrs. Harris in the examination room. Of course he was a physician and it was his business to attend to patients, and if Mrs. Harris was a handsome young widow, that didn't mean she wasn't entitled to his services. But Genevieve found herself resenting it, and pouting when he finally returned to the office to resume work. Her mind kept going back to other occasions when he'd interrupted their moments together to see patients, to interview visitors who wanted to rent lodgings on the second floor. There were always guests coming and going now, for many of the furnished rooms were rented to out-of-towners arriving for the Fair. But oddly enough, the only ones she noticed, patients or lodgers, were the women. The young, attractive women, like Mrs. Harris, who'd taken a room here just the other day. Gordon himself had escorted her to it. And now she wanted medical attention too.

Jealousy, that was what it was. Genevieve had to admit he truth, and she hated herself for it. Because she had no right to be jealous, and she hated that admission too. She was cross with him the rest of the afternoon, and silent over dinner in the apartment that evening. He knew she was out of sorts, but he never said a word. Instead, after they'd finished, he sat down at the organ and played.

It was the first time she had ever heard him play, the first time she had ever heard him sing. The warm, deep, vibrant voice was singing to her. And the song–

Genevieve, sweet Genevieve,
The days may come, the days may go–

When she burst into tears and he rose and put his arms around her she knew, even before he spoke, that he understood and everything would be all right. There were the kisses then, the protestations of love and devotion, the promises and plans for the future, their future together for always and always.

But it wasn't until later–much later, when lying in bed in her room she heard the door click open softly and sensed his shadowy presence–that she was sure. And it was only when he had left that she finally called him Gordon, murmuring the name gently to herself in the dark.

9

THE BANK MANAGER's name was Mr. Kirkadee, and he was very nice. If Genevieve had been alone she would have merely spoken to one of the cashiers at the window and let it go at that, but Gordon was with her and he wouldn't hear of such a thing.

"Always go to the top," he told her. "That's the only way to get things done properly."

And he was right. Mr. Kirkadee invited them into his office and listened to what Gordon had to say, and five minutes later everything had been settled. Gordon drew out his money, she drew out hers and now they had a joint account.

It was wonderful of Gordon to trust her like that. Her piddling little four thousand dollars, all that had been left to her by Uncle Fred, didn't amount to much compared with Gordon's deposit. When she found out he had more than thirty thousand in savings, she began to understand why Mr. Kirkadee had been so cordial. No wonder he had been so gracious to her, too. After all, from today on, all this money was in both their names and she could withdraw it anytime, on just her signature alone.

"And that's what I want you to do, darling," Gordon assured her. "You know how busy I am. It's going to be up to you to buy the trousseau and make arrangements."

They talked about it over coffee at the Palmer House. Genevieve was so excited she could hardly eat. Just before they left, a whole group of men came in and sat down at a big table near the windows, and Gordon told her they were from City Hall; the distinguished-looking gray-haired man with the cigar was Carter Harrison himself. Imagine, having lunch at the same place as the Mayor!

They took a hired hack back to the pharmacy, driving down Michigan most of the way past all the fancy homes. "No more cable cars for you," Gordon told her.

"But it's so expensive!"

He laughed. "Look who's talking about expense! You forget, you have all that money in the bank now. And it's only the beginning." Gordon squeezed her hand. "How would you like a carriage of your own?"

When he bent to kiss her, she blushed and pulled away. "Please—the driver—"

"Don't worry yourself about him. I'm sure he's seen a girl get kissed before. Though never one so beautiful . . ." Gordon's voice trailed off into a whisper meant for her ears alone, and her blush deepened, but she made no resistance when he pressed his lips to hers.

Back in the office, it was hard for her to keep her mind

on business. Gordon had some sort of legal papers for her to sign as witness—something to do with a hospital admission for a patient of his—and there were a dozen letters for her to type up. While she was working, he went out front to consult with Mr. Hickey and check on the day's receipts from the business, and then it was time for him to go over the guest register and see how many overnight lodgers had taken rooms on the second floor during the day. After that he went into the consultation room to keep his afternoon appointments. Genevieve hoped Mrs. Harris wouldn't be showing up today.

Not that she was really concerned about Mrs. Harris anymore. Gordon had reassured her on that score, said she was leaving shortly, and if his words weren't enough to convince her, his actions certainly did. Genevieve found herself trembling as she guided her pen over the scratch pad.

Mrs. G. Gordon Gregg.

Mrs. Genevieve Gregg.

Dr. and Mrs. Gregg.

"Why so formal? Why not just plain 'Gordon and Genevieve'?"

She looked up with a start at the sound of his voice, to find him standing beside her, smiling.

"I'm sorry," she said. "I must have been daydreaming."

"At this hour? It's past six."

And so it was. Genevieve was surprised to see how dark it had gotten. Laughing, Gordon attended to the light.

"Did you finish those letters?"

"Here they are." She handed him the sheaf.

"Good." He nodded approval as he read, then bent over the desk to sign them. While she sorted out the missives and placed them in envelopes, he went out into the shop to say good night to Mr. Hickey and the clerks. Then the food trays arrived from the restaurant and it was time to go upstairs.

Genevieve was glad that Hickey and the boys had left before the waiter came by with their dinners. So far she was sure they didn't suspect that she and Gordon dined together. And they certainly didn't suspect anything else, either. Gordon had seen to that; he was so discreet. It was really amazing the way he managed to separate the various aspects of his life. Genevieve marveled at how very little Hickey seemed to know about the medical practice or the lodging business or the things she attended to here in the office. But then, for that matter, she knew next to nothing about the pharmacy.

"It's better that way," Gordon told her over their meal that evening. "Less confusing if everyone tends to his own affairs."

"But how do you manage to keep up with it all?"

"Organization, that's the secret. Plus a regular intake of the Elixir for extra energy." He got up and went over to the serving table. "Which reminds me, young lady—time for your daily dosage."

He turned, extending the glass to her. Genevieve drank quickly, wrinkling her nose at the acrid scent. Funny how the Elixir affected her. At times it tasted almost like ordinary water; then again there were occasions when it seemed to have a bitter flavor. She'd mentioned it to Gordon and he explained it was all a matter of body chemistry. The bitterness was most apt to be noticeable when one was overly fatigued. And come to think of it, Genevieve almost always felt tired after a bitter drink. Apparently she didn't have Gordon's almost inexhaustible stamina. Yet she'd been so excited today, so stimulated. Perhaps that was it; the excitement had drained her vitality.

"Now off you go," Gordon said.

"So soon?"

"It's past nine. You've had a long day." He led her to the little private office at the rear of the apartment and opened the door of the walk-in safe. Which wasn't a safe at all, just a false front he'd put in to fool burglars, Gordon had explained—though how any burglars could possibly find their way through all the staircases and corridors was beyond her. Still, it was clever of him to provide a way of getting into and out of the apartment when he wanted privacy; beyond the false safe door was a short staircase to the second floor. Genevieve herself had learned to use this route when returning to her room after a night upstairs.

But she wouldn't be doing so this evening, and her disappointment was dulled only by the realization that Gordon was right: she really felt extremely tired. Going down the stairs she almost stumbled, and Gordon took her arm, not relinquishing it until they passed along the corridor below and arrived at the door of her room.

She started to fumble for her key, but he was already fitting his own into the lock.

"Here we are," he murmured, stepping aside as he pushed open the door for her to precede him.

When he followed her into the room she turned and came into his arms, but his hands were gentle on her shoulders and he shook his head, smiling.

"You need your rest."

"What about you?"

"Don't trouble yourself. I've more than enough to do." His eyes met hers, searching her face intently. "Poor dear, you're exhausted."

And it was true; the drowsiness was suddenly acute, and

his face was blurring before her. Her knees felt weak, and only his eyes sustained her. She wondered if she'd have the strength to undress.

As if he had divined her thought, Gordon's hands moved beneath her waist; she felt herself being lifted and carried over to the bed.

"Here, let me tuck you in." His face was shadowed, but in the slit of light fanning through the doorway from the hall beyond she could see his eyes, grave and gentle and ever so bright. Then, as he smoothed the pillow underneath her head and drew up the coverlet over her, his eyes began to blur. His voice blurred, too, coming from far away—far away . . .

"You'll sleep now. Sleep and rest. Sleep and rest."

He may have said something more, but she no longer heard. And when he bent to kiss her, she felt nothing but the faintest phantom of a touch; it was the kiss of a shadow. A shadow that stole away, closed the door softly and left her alone in the dark. Alone with the shadow that was herself sleeping and dreaming.

Dreaming of Gordon's eyes and Gordon's face and Gordon's hands caressing, and other hands writing *Mrs. G. Gordon Gregg* over all the doors and all the walls and all the corridors that led up to the bed where the eyes watched and waited for the coming of the bride, the bride of shadows in the black veil, mounting to the bridal bed where black candles burned—and suddenly rough hands reached out to her, pulling her cruelly, not like Gordon at all and suddenly she screamed.

No. Shadows don't scream. And she wasn't a shadow; she was awake, sitting bolt upright in her bed. Not screaming, but hearing a scream.

Then the room was silent. Not even an echo, only the sound of her hoarse breathing.

Genevieve shook her head. A nightmare. That was what it was: she'd had a nightmare. Screaming or hearing a scream—either way it didn't matter, because it was just her imagination.

Then came the thump. And that wasn't imagination: she was awake now, and she heard it. A single dull thud, from directly overhead.

Overhead was Gordon's bedroom . . .

Genevieve was wide awake now, but as she swung her legs over the side of the bed to rise she almost toppled, her knees buckling. And when she groped her way to the door in darkness, her head was swimming. Her hands clawed at the door, but she scarcely felt its wooden surface. Her fingers were numb, her legs were numb and only her fear was alive—alive and frantic within her as she reeled out into the deserted hallway where the gaslight flickered like the flaming tip of the candle, like the eye in her dream, like Gordon's eyes when he told her to sleep . . .

Gordon. Something's happened to Gordon . . .

The fear had found its voice within her; the fear gave her its strength, and she moved along the corridor to the blind, unnumbered door leading to the staircase behind. The staircase was dark and shadowy, and for a moment she was once again a shadow; all she need do was surrender to sleep and silence. *Sleep and rest.* She could hear Gordon's voice whispering the words ever so sweetly, but the phrase itself was sweet no longer; it was bitter like the taste of the Elixir on her tongue. And she wasn't a shadow, she was real, this was real, and the danger . . .

Danger at the top of the stairs. Danger behind the door set so securely and invisibly in the paneled wall upon the landing. Genevieve halted there before it, striving to sense sound. There was a gasp. A gasp, and a rustling.

For a moment she stood frozen with fear—until she realized that the gasps of exertion issued from her own throat, the rustle had been the movement of her gown. Numb no longer, she moved forward, pressing against the concealed corners of the door until it swung inward and revealed the little lighted office beyond.

Cautiously, she peered across the threshold, but the room was empty. She entered slowly, started to turn toward the hall entry leading into the apartment beyond. It was then that she glimpsed the moving figure out of the corner of her eye and pivoted in panic.

The red-and-blue horror was the flayed body of a man—but it was only a life-sized representation, the colored anatomy chart on the wall. It swayed slightly in the draft from the doorway, and for a moment the tangled skein of arteries and veins seemed to writhe and twist like serpents. The empty eye sockets glared, the fleshless face grinned and Genevieve turned away blindly and hurried down the hall.

Through the alcove entryway she could see the parlor bright before her, the carpet rich and red, the flames flickering in the fireplace, and on the walls the ornate oils. Laughing cavaliers lifting gilded goblets in a toast to their ladies . . .

Genevieve saw the wineglasses on the table. The half-empty wineglasses, two of them, crystal sparkling in the firelight. But the room was empty. Of course it would be. The sounds she'd heard in her sleep had come from directly overhead.

She crossed the blood-red carpet, moving past the fireplace as the flames crackled and hissed at her, came to the open doorway beyond. And saw, in the dim light of the bedroom, the grotesque, weaving, wild-eyed shape that was herself. Herself, staring open-mouthed at the rumpled bedsheets, and that dress, the green satin.

Memory flashed before her. The tall, laughing creature with the hazel eyes, chattering away about her plans for visiting the Fair as Gordon escorted her up to a room on the second floor. The creature who came to him later for her medical "consultation," still wearing the dress. *Mrs. Harris.*

She shook her head to clear it. The room was deserted. And what she saw was only a figment of her imagination. It was what she'd heard that was real. Not a laugh but a scream. Genevieve's eyes sought the shadows in the corners of the room. She turned and the room turned with her. Giddy, she told herself; you're going to faint.

But she took a deep breath and the whirling ceased. She mustn't give way now, not when Gordon was in danger. *If* he was in danger.

Think. You have to think. Where could they have gone?

Genevieve stumbled across the room, following the wall. No doors here, unless they were hidden—and the wall felt solid to her touch, the flawed touch of numbed fingers. Then the vast, smooth expanse of the mirror, the mocking mirror with its image of a frightened face gaping in anguished bewilderment. Beyond it, to one side, the open doorway of the bathroom.

She felt the cool draft at her ankles, coiling and curling, and sensed its source. Peering into the dimness past the doorway, she saw it—saw the black square in the floor beyond the turned-back rug and the open trapdoor.

She forced herself forward, into the room—forced herself to stand, swaying over the big black hole that was like the opening of a grave. But graves are not square, and no draft issues from their depths. She peered over the edge, dizziness coming in waves as she discerned the faint outline of wooden steps slanting down into the darkness of the open shaft. And there, on the topmost step, a single pale white eye stared upward.

No, not an eye. An earring. A pearl earring.

An earring like an eye that stared and blinked and beckoned. Like Gordon's eye gazing at her and commanding her to sleep. She wanted to sleep now, even if the sleep brought nightmares, for even a nightmare was preferable to this reality. Someone had come upon them and carried them away, carried them down into the cold darkness of—what?

She had to know. She couldn't, but she had to. More waves now, dizziness and nausea both, but she gulped and gripped the ice-cold iron rails on either side of the steps as she clambered down into the dark—edging cautiously, slowly finding a firm foothold. Peering until she saw the dim light far below. Far below, then not so far—only a few more steps now, and then the solid surface of the passageway, where a single gas jet flared fitfully to shred the shadows.

What passageway was this? Something low and narrow and faced with rough boards, leading off in one direction to another door, plain unpainted board, set squarely in the wall.

Again she hesitated. Walking down that passageway was like walking in her sleep; she could feel sleep all around her, clinging to her body, tugging at her arms and legs, coating her in cotton wool that was warm and soft. It would be so easy to sink down into the warmth. Gordon wanted her to sleep, the Elixir wanted her to sleep—perhaps she *was* sleeping, and this was only another part of the dream.

Something clanged—a muffled, hollow sound, faint and faraway. But she heard it. She wasn't asleep; the sound was real coming from somewhere beyond the door. Her hand went out and pushed against the unpainted board.

It swung back to reveal the stairwell, the stone stairwell, not dark but bathed in a sickly yellowish light that came from below. She heard the clang again echoing upward. It was real, she'd heard it, and she had to know. If it was too much for her, if the danger was real, she could always go back.

First, the stairs. Easier now, with the stone surface beneath her tread, even though the giddiness was returning in widening waves so that she had to blink constantly to clear her vision. Her throat was dry and she breathed the cool air. No other sound but that and the faint scrape of her footsteps as she reached the corridor below.

So many steps. She must have descended a long way—this had to be the cellar. But where were the furnace, the coal bin, the pipes? Was this a basement, or had the trapdoor been the entrance to a tunnel? No, that was imagination again, and this was real: this stone-walled tunnel lined with the dancing yellow flames of the gas jets. And there was a real door at the far end, a solid oak door.

Dizzy. So dizzy. Best to turn back now. But the stairs. She couldn't climb the stairs. And go through the passageway to the other stairs and come out at last into the bedroom, the empty bedroom. It was impossible, and she'd already come too far: she had to know. The flames flickered and faded, then flickered up again as she passed before them, hand extended to the corridor wall. Only a few steps more now and she would be at the door. Even then it wouldn't be too late, she told herself. She could still turn back.

Genevieve glanced down, shaking her head. Her vision cleared. There was light ahead. Not the light from the gas jet on the walls, but from another source. It streamed across the floor from beneath the oaken door at the corridor's end.

She halted before it, listening, half-expectant, half-afraid.

But there was no scream, no thud, no clang, no sound at all. Only the shining steady shaft of light streaming in warm and reassuring radiance from under the door.

Taking a deep breath, Genevieve reached out and opened the door.

10

WHEN DARKNESS DESCENDED, the District shook off its slumber and came alive. Like some great beast it stirred and stretched slowly, savoring the promise of the night. Pawnshop mouths with steel gratings like serrated teeth were flung open to fasten upon the unwary. Saloons began a brisk business behind their loosely hung swinging doors. Yellow lights were turned on in the windows of shabby rooming houses, and the red lamps were set to burn over the doorways of the brothels.

Since the Fair, it seemed everyone wanted to see the District—the rich arriving with the clop and clatter of carriages, the less savory specimens on foot. And the District's denizens waited to welcome them: waited with dazzling displays of diamonds in the pawnshops, phony as the protestations of their proprietors; waited with frantic fingers, deftly plucking the purses of drunken dudes; waited in shadows with blackjacks, billy clubs and brass knuckles; waited in brightly blazing bars with knockout drops; waited in the cribs and the panel houses with the private parlors with smiles and spirochetes. It really didn't matter which door the visitor chose. In the end, the beast engulfed them all.

Shortly after ten o'clock, Crystal emerged from the cool confines of the Catholic church into the sweltering summer night. She stood half-concealed by the corner of the entrance, shadows shielding her from the gaze of passersby, and stared across Clark Street. Here, between Polk and Taylor, was the heart of the District. Ignoring the venders, the shills and barkers braying beside the saloon doors, her attention was focused on the one imposing edifice directly across from the church: the three-story brownstone building, the massive mansion with its windows sedately shuttered against the night. No light, red or otherwise, burned above its discreet door, and in the darkness it was difficult to discern the silvery bars of the cage that swung beside it.

But Crystal knew the cage was there, knew what it contained: the parrot. The great green parrot, Pretty Polly, preening on its perch and screeching, "Carrie Watson—come in, gentlemen!" For this was 441 Clark Street, the fabulous 441. Carrie Watson's place, the finest and most famous parlor house in the world.

Charlie Hogan had told her all about it. "Fifty girls," he had said. "Can you imagine that? They say Vina Fields has more than that over on Custom House Place, but they're all colored. You won't find any tramps working for Carrie; every girl wears an evening gown, no bad language allowed, no drunks. Most of 'em speak French, and they drink nothing but wine, at ten dollars a bottle. Not out of glasses, mind you. Golden goblets, that's Carrie's style."

Golden goblets? Crystal found it a little hard to believe. But her editor wasn't joking.

"Pity you can't get inside for a look-see. Five parlors in the place, just crammed with fancy furniture imported from Paris. Rugs on the floor you can sink in up to your ankles. Orchestra playing every night—no cheap piano professors for Carrie. There's a billiard room, too, though I never heard of anyone who went to 441 for a game of pool. And now they say she has a bowling alley in the basement!"

"And upstairs?" Crystal asked.

"Must be twenty-five bedrooms. Silk sheets, private baths, the works." Hogan shrugged. "That's what they tell me, anyway. Wouldn't know for sure myself."

Crystal had suppressed her smile, but she couldn't control her comment. "You mean to tell me she doesn't cater to the press?"

Charlie Hogan grinned. "Carrie caters to anyone with the price. They say if anybody walks up to the front door with less than fifty dollars in his jeans, that parrot of hers will reach out and bite him.

"Twenty years in the trade, running wide-open through every administration. And now, with the Fair on, business has doubled. Can you imagine how rich that woman is?"

Crystal could indeed imagine, but she wasn't satisfied with sheer speculation. It was the desire for firsthand observation that had brought her down to Clark Street that day, to station herself in the semisanctuary of the church entrance across the street, waiting for a guarded glimpse of 441's proprietress.

When it came, she got more than she had bargained for.

She was prepared for the sight of the plump, peroxided woman in the silken gown, the fingers festooned with diamond rings to match the sparkle of wrist and throat and earlobes. But the huge white carriage with golden wheels, the coal-black horses and coachman in scarlet splendor—here was opulence that Mrs. Potter Palmer herself might envy.

Yes, Carrie Watson was a rich woman, and her clients were wealthy too. Wealthy and important. And it was to see the clients that Crystal had returned, to stand here in the shadows of the church to which—so rumor had it—Carrie Watson so lavishly contributed out of the goodness of her heart. If there was going to be a story about vice in Chicago—a real eye-opener—it wouldn't consist of descriptions of Carrie's carriage or even the solid-silver wine buckets inside her house. The story, Crystal told herself, was in the people who patronized the place.

Cupping a tiny note pad inconspicuously in her hand, she stood watch, pencil poised, as hacks and hansoms halted before Carrie's doorway. They came in steadily increasing numbers as the hour wore on, the carriages were backed up along the curb almost as though part of a parade. And like a parade, they conveyed celebrities, displayed dignitaries. Amid the pleasure-bound procession that poured past the portals, Crystal recognized the prominent faces and paunches of a LaSalle Street banker, a wealthy stockbroker, the son of a downtown department-store owner, a local alderman and a visiting Grand Duke from one of those Balkan countries slightly smaller than the territory controlled by the alderman. And then, with a whoop and a holler, a stagecoach clattered to a halt before the place and disgorged half of the star performers of the Buffalo Bill show.

"Carrie Watson's—come in, gentlemen!" squawked the

parrot. But Crystal scarcely heard it above the whooping of the Wild Westerners. She felt sorry for the bird; with all these customers to greet, it must be growing hoarse.

As for Crystal, her feet were getting tired, and she really had enough by now, enough names on her little note pad to make a big story. Besides, the passing pedestrians were beginning to lurch rather than walk; if she wanted to move away without notice, she'd better go before some drunken masher spotted her and made trouble.

Crystal turned and started forward into the street. And it was then that the shadow loomed up beside her.

"Hey—wait a minute—!"

Waiting was the last thing she intended to do. Ignoring the voice, Crystal quickened her pace, then froze as she felt the heavy hand on her shoulder.

She turned instantly, raising her purse. It was just a small handbag into which she'd dropped her pencil and note pad, but it also contained a tightly wrapped roll of silver dollars, stashed away against just such an emergency. One swing, and when that roll connected with somebody's jaw . . .

Crystal swung.

And the somebody caught her wrist.

"I said to wait!"

She turned, blinked and stared up into the frowning face of Jim Frazer.

"What are you doing here?" she muttered.

"Looking for you." He released his grip, and her hand dropped. "I stopped by your office tonight. Charlie Hogan told me—"

Crystal sighed. "Charlie Hogan has a big mouth."

"And a good thing he does, for your sake." Jim focused his frown on the street. "What on earth got into you, coming here? Just look at this mob!"

"That's exactly what I've been doing." Crystal tapped her purse. "I've got a list of names here that will raise eyebrows all over town. Just wait until you read them in the paper."

"Lucky I found you before I had to read your obituary."

"Don't be such a spoilsport."

"You call this sport?" Jim gestured impatiently. "Taking your life in your hands just to stand here gawking at these hooligans? At this hour of the night, too. No decent person would be found dead around here!"

Crystal glanced across the street, her eyes narrowing. "Oh, wouldn't they?"

"What are you talking about?"

"See for yourself."

Jim turned to follow her gaze.

A carriage was pulling away from the entrance to 441, and the passenger it had deposited on the walk moved up to the doorway.

"Carrie Watson's," croaked the parrot. The rest of the greeting was lost as the door swung open to admit the arriving guest. For a moment his smiling face was fully visible in the light streaming forth from the hall beyond.

"Isn't that your friend?" Crystal murmured.

"Well I'll be damned . . ."

Together they stared at the midnight visitor until the door of the brothel closed behind him. Almost automatically, Crystal reached into her purse for pencil and pad, then added one last name to her list. *G. Gordon Gregg.*

11

JIM WAS SITTING at his desk in the office the next morning when Mr. Follansbee walked in with a letter in his hand.

"You busy right now, Frazer?"

"Just finishing up these application forms for the Hamilton policy. I'll have them in the mail before lunch."

"Got anything lined up for this afternoon?"

"Not yet. I was thinking of making a few calls out around Garfield Park."

"That can wait. Here, read this."

Follansbee handed him the letter. Just a routine memo from the home office, and Jim scanned it quickly. Some policyholder named Evers had died in March, leaving a thousand-dollar paid-up ordinary life claim. Since the named beneficiary was also deceased, the Company had sought to locate next of kin. Upon investigation it appeared that Evers' legal heir was now a resident of Chicago, employed as a private secretary by—

Jim looked up, frowning, and the old man nodded.

"That's right. Dr. Gregg, the same fellow we paid off two months ago on that ten-thousand double-indemnity claim on his wife. There's a coincidence for you."

Jim wondered what Follansbee would say if he heard about the other coincidence last night, and quickly checked the impulse to mention it. Instead he handed the letter back to his employer.

"What's the problem?" he asked.

Follansbee scowled. "I don't know. I just talked to Gregg on the telephone and I can't make head or tail out of what he told me. I want you to see him this afternoon and get this thing straightened out. Here—take the letter with you."

Jim took the letter, folded it, put it in his wallet.

That afternoon, shortly past lunchtime, he unfolded the letter again and handed it to Dr. G. Gordon Gregg in his office behind the dispensary. Gregg was wearing a linen suit today; his shirt was immaculate, with collar and cuffs stiffly starched. But the man himself looked a trifle wilted, and once again Jim found himself curbing the impulse to mention his glimpse of Gregg last night. But after all, if a lonely widower chose to frequent a parlor house in search of diversion, that was his own business.

Jim's business was with the letter, and he watched Gregg as he read it. He waited for a nod or a frown of bewilderment, but Gregg's face was impassive as he finished his perusal and handed the Company communication back to his visitor.

"I take it this is what your Mr. Follansbee read to me over

the telephone this morning," he said. "There was really no need for you to inconvenience yourself by bringing it out to me."

Jim shook his head. "You don't understand, sir. I wanted to make sure it reached the next of kin, Genevieve Bolton. She's now the legal beneficiary—"

"I'm aware of that." Gregg sighed. "And I'm afraid Mr. Follansbee is the one who doesn't understand. As I attempted to explain during our conversation this morning, Miss Bolton isn't available at the moment."

"She no longer works for you?"

"I didn't say that. She happens to be out of the city at the present time." Gregg smiled. "It's a private matter."

"Would you mind telling me how I might get in touch with her?"

"That won't be necessary. I expect her back soon."

"How soon?"

"Within the next week or so. Until then she has asked me to keep track of any messages or communications and act on her behalf." Gregg extended his hand. "If you'd like me to hold this letter for Miss Bolton until she returns—"

"I'm not following you."

"Neither did your employer." Gregg shrugged. "Look, I have no wish to indulge in mystification. It's merely that I've never met Mr. Follansbee, and I have an aversion to discussing personal matters with a stranger. But since you and I are acquainted, perhaps I can impose upon your confidence without embarrassing either Miss Bolton or myself."

"What are you talking about?"

Gregg's voice and glance lowered. "The truth is, Genevieve and I are engaged to be married."

"Married?"

"It's an awkward situation, I know—only a matter of

months since Millicent's passing. And under the circumstances, I intended to make no public announcement for some while to come. That is why I was reluctant to reveal Genevieve's whereabouts to Mr. Follansbee." Gregg rose. "But you might tell him that the young lady is presently away settling her personal affairs and will return shortly. If he will be good enough to be patient and refrain from divulging this information until that time—"

"I'm sure he'll respect your confidence."

"Good." Gregg held out his hand. "I'm much obliged to you for your consideration."

"Not at all." Jim turned, then glanced back. "But you will notify us when your fiancée returns? The Company is anxious to close its file, and we'll need her signature before we can authorize payment."

"I understand." Gregg nodded, walking to the door. "And I assure you there'll be no further problems."

"No further problems. What is that supposed to mean?" Crystal demanded. They were sitting on the front porch of her rooming house on Prairie Avenue that evening, and her voice rose impatiently over the drowsy stillness of the deserted street. "Have you told your boss about this yet?"

"No; by the time I got back to the office he'd left for the day."

"Thank goodness for that!"

"What are you talking about?"

"You. Your job, your future—both of which you can kiss goodbye forever if you come to him with a cock-and-bull story like this."

"I'm sorry," Jim muttered. "I don't follow you."

"Perhaps it would be better if you had. If there was a touch of the newspaper reporter in your blood, you'd have done what I did this morning. The minute I set eyes on Gregg last night I decided to do some checking."

"But why—how—?"

"The why part is perfectly obvious. When you see a supposedly respectable physician, a man who has just suffered the loss of his beloved wife, entering the most notorious and expensive brothel in town, you can hardly assume he's paying a professional visit. Instead, you begin to wonder just how respectable he is after all."

"Now, wait a minute. You're a woman—you don't understand that a man has certain needs."

"I assure you I passed my biology course with highest marks." Crystal put her hand on Jim's arm. "It was not his presence that surprised me. It was his manner—the way he swaggered into that place, the smile on his face, the brazen eagerness of the man."

"You really have a thing about Dr. Gregg, don't you?"

"What if I do?"

"Just because you take a dislike to someone, that's no reason to be suspicious of his actions."

"I know that. Which is why I did some investigating this morning, in the morgue."

"Morgue?"

"The newspaper files, silly. Your Dr. Gregg has had his share of publicity. There have been several feature articles on that castle he built during the past year—a story about his plans, and a follow-up several months later on the construction itself. The place was the talk of the neighborhood, almost as exciting as the construction job on the Fair."

"I'll admit it's rather gaudy. But if he chose to build it you can hardly accuse him of anything except bad taste."

"Not unless you follow the leads in the stories. Which is what I did. There were certain names mentioned—contractors, construction companies, building and lumber suppliers. I made a few calls. A Mr. Rogowsky, a Mr. Schultz, O. P. Denning and Company. All of them worked on the castle at one time or another. None of them have yet been paid. I understand from Mr. Denning that he intends to bring suit."

"There are plenty of business and professional men who are delinquent in settling obligations. Perhaps he was strapped for cash."

"Maybe he was. But not now. You handed him a check for ten thousand dollars two months ago. What did he do with that money?"

"I don't know."

"I do. But we won't go into that now." Crystal frowned. "Are you aware of the fact that Dr. Gregg used to work in another pharmacy, just across the street from the present site of his castle? He was getting forty dollars a week from the owner of the place, a widow named Phyllis Callahan. And he wasn't calling himself a physician then, just a druggist. The first time he made use of his medical degree was when he signed Phyllis Callahan's death certificate, two years ago. And again, a year later, when he turned in the final papers as executor and sole beneficiary of her will."

"How'd you find that out?"

"Cook County Courthouse. It's all there. Cause of death: cardiac arrest. Meaning her heart stopped, which is generally the case when someone dies."

"You're not implying—"

"No, just reporting facts. And here's another. Gregg's inheritance came to about sixteen thousand dollars. He used the money to buy the land across the street for his castle. Incidentally, he paid for it promptly; the price was around sixteen thousand dollars."

"What's wrong with that?"

"Nothing. Only he had already made inquiries about the price of the land a month before Phyllis Callahan's death."

"Perhaps he was acting for her. Maybe they had planned to build the place together." Jim frowned. "You're jumping to conclusions."

"Good exercise." Crystal smiled, then sobered. "You've got to admit it all seems just a little too, shall we say, convenient."

"All right, suppose I go along with you. Even if there *is* something fishy about Gregg's past record, it still has nothing to do with Genevieve Bolton."

"No, but this has." Crystal leaned forward, placing her hand on Jim's arm. "Remember when I went out to Gregg's place with you, the time you gave him his check? You told me he had a secretary in his office then. You even mentioned her name—Alice, wasn't it?"

"That's right."

"Well, where is she now?"

"Hold on, Crystal, let's not go overboard on this thing. Hasn't it ever occurred to you that he may have fired her?"

"Maybe he did. And maybe Mrs. Callahan actually died of a heart attack. But under the circumstances, I wouldn't take anything for granted."

"You still haven't told me anything that would account for Genevieve Bolton's being involved."

"Account, that's the word." Crystal said. "Remember my asking what Gregg did with that ten thousand you gave him? After I found out about his creditors, I got curious concerning his financial affairs. Of course I couldn't ask around, but it isn't hard for a newspaper to get a credit statement on somebody—the advertising department does it every day, whenever a merchant wants to buy space. I've done a few favors for Andy Pokras, our business manager, so he did one for me."

Crystal fished in her pocket and pulled out a crumpled slip of paper. "Here, take a look at this. Your Dr. Gregg has a balance of thirty-four thousand eight hundred dollars on deposit at the Kirkadee Trust and Savings Bank, a special joint account, payable on demand with the signature of either party. The name of the other party is Genevieve Bolton."

Jim took a deep breath. "What do you want me to do?"

Crystal shook her head. "Isn't it obvious? Go to Mr. Follansbee and tell him what I've just told you. Leave me out of it. I've got my notes written down on all this, and I'll give them to you. Let him think you did the investigating."

"I don't know—"

"Oh, Jim, can't you see? This is your big chance! Take Mr. Follansbee out to see Gregg. Let the two of you insist that he produce Genevieve Bolton."

"But I couldn't do a thing like that."

Crystal smiled. "You already have," she said softly.

"What do you mean?"

"I called Dr. Gregg just before I left for home tonight. I said I was your secretary and told him you and Mr. Follansbee would see him at his office. Your appointment is for ten o'clock tomorrow morning."

12

G. Gordon Gregg was quite calm. He was wearing white again today, and he sat in the hot, stuffy office like a figure carved from a block of ice. His smile was icy too, and his eyes were cold as he listened to his visitors.

It was Jim who felt the heat, his palms sweating and his collar wet. Thank God that Follansbee had decided to do most of the talking. He did a good job, Jim had to admit. The old man was no fool; he knew his way around, and the way he put the questions to Gregg was a caution. The Dearborn Mutual Life Assurance Company needed assistance in locating Miss Bolton—Dr. Gregg would be rendering a great service if he could furnish a few more details regarding her association with him. How long had she been employed here? Under what circumstances had she come to apply for a position? Where had she been residing during her period of employment? And could he possibly be a bit more specific regarding her exact whereabouts during the past two weeks?

The more Follansbee talked, the more Jim realized that he was trying to paint Gregg into a corner. Yet Jim, watching, could not relax. Follansbee's voice was dry, but Jim's palms stayed wet.

Because G. Gordon Gregg was still quite calm. "Really, gentlemen," he said. "I'm sorry to have put you all to this trouble. If I'd had any idea you attached so much importance to a simple leave of absence . . ."

He shrugged, reached into a desk drawer, pulled out a folder and opened it. "About Miss Bolton, I have her employment record here." He scanned the contents of the folder as he spoke. "Let me see now. I called Miss Garland's College of Business on July seventh and spoke to a Mrs. Prothero, in charge of placements, regarding my secretarial requirements. They selected Miss Bolton as an applicant for the position, and I interviewed her on the afternoon of July eighth. I engaged her immediately, at a salary of twenty dollars a week."

Again Gregg glanced at the papers before him. "According to this, she was then residing at a boardinghouse at 1921 South Dearborn. I suggested that she might find it more convenient if she took a room here on the premises—as you probably know, I do have rooms to let upstairs—and she agreed. She moved in on July tenth and stayed until her departure on August the nineteenth." He flipped the folder shut again. "As I told Mr. Frazer the other day, she had personal affairs to settle."

"Speaking of personal affairs," said Follansbee. "It has

come to the Company's attention that on August eighteenth, the day before her departure, Miss Bolton withdrew the sum of four thousand dollars from the Kirkadee Trust and Savings Bank."

Gregg nodded. "As a matter of fact, she did. Inasmuch as we plan to marry, we decided it would be more convenient to share a joint account together." He reached into the bottom drawer of his desk and withdrew a small red-leather passbook. "Just for the record, you might want to examine this."

Follansbee took the passbook, looking grim. As he opened and inspected it, his frown deepened.

"You'll note the total deposited on that date—thirty-four thousand eight hundred, isn't it? As you see, the entire sum is still intact."

Follansbee nodded, handing the passbook back to Gregg.

"Now, if you have no further questions, gentlemen—"

"Just one." Follansbee was still frowning. "You still haven't told us where Miss Bolton is now."

"That is correct. As her fiancé, I consider any further discussion of her affairs an invasion of privacy."

"I understand." Follansbee nodded. "But the Company has expressly asked me to—"

"Ah, yes, the Company." Gregg's voice was calm, but for an instant Jim fancied he detected a glint of mockery in his eyes. "Very well, then. Under the circumstances, I imagine a breach of confidence is indicated. Genevieve is presently in Kansas City. Kansas City, Missouri, to be precise."

"Did she furnish you with a forwarding address, by any chance?"

"I'm sorry to say she did not. At the time she resided in the area, she lived with her uncle on a farm outside of town. He didn't own the property—he was working it on shares—

and when he died it passed into other hands. But Genevieve did plan to go there and dispose of furniture and household effects that were still in storage. That was the purpose of her trip."

"I see." Follansbee pursed his lips. "But you don't know where she might be at the moment."

Gregg shook his head. "I didn't say that. I merely told you she left no fowarding address, because she wasn't sure where she might be staying after she arrived. Of course I know where she is now. She's at the Kansas House."

As he spoke, Gregg dipped into the bottom drawer once again. "If it's any help to you, her letter arrived just this morning."

Follansbee inspected the envelope, then extracted and unfolded its contents. Jim rose and peered over his shoulder at the single typewritten sheet on hotel stationery.

My Dearest:

A thousand apologies for this long delay in writing, but I've been so terribly busy. First of all, the man who owns the farm property was out of town, and it took me almost a week to locate him. Now I have a key and his permission to remove our belongings, but you wouldn't believe what a mess everything is in. I'm going to try and sort things out, then pack what I want to keep and try to sell the rest, including all the furniture.

I'm afraid it may take longer than I anticipated, but I'll be back as soon as possible. Meanwhile please don't worry about me. I will keep you informed of what happens. Do take good care of yourself for your loving

Genevieve

Follansbee read slowly, as if to memorize the message, then studied the scrawled signature. He turned to glance up at Jim, and there was no mistaking the meaning of his gaze: *You got me into this; now what do you have to say?*

There was no escape. Jim turned to Gregg.

"I wonder, could you possibly show us anything in your files here containing Miss Bolton's signature?"

Gregg wasn't smiling now. "That's a highly irregular request."

Follansbee wasn't smiling either. But Jim couldn't back away. He gestured at Gregg. "I'm aware of that, sir. It's just that—"

"It's just that you are questioning the authenticity of this communication, are you not?" Gregg rose, went to the file and turned to display a handful of correspondence. "Here. I'm sure you'll find a dozen or more specimens of Genevieve's handwriting in these office memos, including her signature."

Jim started to reach for the memos, but Gregg shook his head. "On second thought, what purpose would they serve? You'd probably accuse me of forgery."

Jim felt himself reddening. "Nobody's accusing you."

"Not at all, this entire visit of yours is an accusation. An accusation and an insult."

"Please." Follansbee rose, shaking his head. "I think this has gone far enough."

"On the contrary." Gregg turned to him, cold-eyed. "I will not be satisfied unless it goes a great deal further. All the way to Kansas City, to be precise."

"What are you saying?"

"Here." Gregg held out Genevieve Bolton's letter. "You'll find a telephone number on the stationery of the hotel. I want you to place a call to that number now."

"I'm sure that won't be necessary," Follansbee muttered.

"I think it is. In fact, I insist."

The cold eyes followed Follansbee to the wall telephone and stayed riveted on him through the entire five minutes of crackling and buzzing it took to complete the connection.

"Kansas House?" Mr. Follansbee's voice rose unconsciously, as though a long-distance call made it imperative to shout. "Could I speak to Miss Genevieve Bolton, please?" He paused, frowning, and both his hesitation and his scowl made Jim's heart leap in hope. "Bolton. B-o-l-t-o-n."

A moment of silence. Jim's heart was pounding now. And then—

"Hello, Miss Bolton," said Mr. Follansbee.

Jim turned away, unable to meet his employer's glare. As he did so, he found himself confronting Gregg. And Gregg was smiling again.

13

SATURDAY AFTERNOON was a busy time at the corner of 58th and Prairie. Bicyclists in puffed sleeves pedaled past the cigar-store Indian on the sidewalk; gigs, sulkies, victorias and four-in-hands moved swiftly along the center of the street. The scissors grinder pushed his cart along the pavement, tinkling its bell at each turn of the wheels, frowning at the competition of the junk wagon clattering in the street beside him as its derbied driver's voice rose in the familiar chant.

"Any rags, any bones, any bottles today?"

In the gutter a barefooted boy guided the movements of his hoop past a hitching post with a skillfully wielded stick, dodging the wheels of the ice wagon parked before Simon's Meat Market. His mother emerged from the butcher shop carrying Sunday's dinner under her arm in a brown paper wrapping, its combed, beaked head dangling down.

At the intersection a hurdy-gurdy droned discordantly as the organ grinder's monkey chattered and capered at the end of its chain, doffing a green velveteen skullcap and lifting a battered tin cup toward passersby.

Ignoring it all, Crystal stood staring at Jim, squinting against the sunshine.

"Fired you?" she murmured.

Jim nodded morosely. "The moment he put down the telephone, right there in Gregg's office."

"Are you sure it wasn't just for Gregg's benefit?"

Jim shook his head. "After we got outside he really let me have it. About making a fool of him, putting the reputation of the Company in jeopardy. He said Dr. Gregg would be perfectly within his rights to bring suit."

Crystal made a face. "Your boss is an idiot."

"My ex-boss."

"What are you going to do about it?"

Jim shrugged. "Start looking for another job."

"You're going to walk away as though the whole thing never happened?"

"I wish it never had." Jim took her arm as they rounded the corner and started along Prairie Avenue to the north. "Look, honey, I'm not blaming you—"

"But it was my fault."

"Forget it. What's done is done. Now, don't worry, I'll get something. I'll read the ads in tomorrow's paper."

"Jim, you're not fooling me for a minute. What you really want is to get your job back, isn't it?"

Jim nodded slowly. "Maybe I could wait a few days and give Follansbee a chance to cool off. Then if I'd go to him and apologize—"

"Not on your life! He's the one who owes you an apology, humiliating you in front of that charlatan. I can see your precious Dr. Gregg now, grinning and gloating over the way he hornswoggled you both."

"Hornswoggled?" Jim gestured impatiently. "The man is perfectly innocent."

"Bushwah! Just because he hasn't taken any money from that joint account doesn't mean he can't draw it out tomorrow or anytime he chooses. As for the letter he showed you, how do you know Genevieve Bolton really wrote it?"

"But Mr. Follansbee spoke to the girl! She's the one who suggested mailing the claim form directly to her so she could sign it and get the money without putting him to any more trouble."

"That's what bothers me. Why wouldn't she wait until she returns?"

Jim halted before the front stoop of the rooming house, stepping aside as two youths in the uniform of the Morgan Park Military Academy sauntered along the sidewalk in adolescent arrogance. "What difference does it make?" he said.

"All the difference in the world. The difference between you being fired in disgrace or having your job back. If you ask me, there's still something fishy about this whole affair. I told you what I found out about Gregg. That man's a thoroughgoing scoundrel, and no mistake."

"No use, Crystal. The whole thing was a mistake, from start to finish."

"It's not finished yet." Crystal started toward the rooming-house entrance as Jim stared after her.

"Wait a minute, aren't we having dinner tonight at the Fair?"

"I'm sorry. Why don't you go on ahead? I'll meet you at six, at the Stoney Island Gate."

"Crystal, if you're up to something—"

She turned and smiled. "Oh, in all the excitement, I forgot to tell you."

"Tell me what?"

"I got fired yesterday too."

"You're joking."

"Believe me, if you heard the language Hogan used, you wouldn't think it was a joke."

"Aren't you going to tell me how it happened?"

Crystal shook her head. "There isn't time for that now."

"But what are you going to do?"

She paused for a moment in the doorway. "What I should have done in the first place. You'll see."

14

At four o'clock on a Saturday afternoon, the barbershop of the Palmer House was always crowded. Regular customers kept their appointments for haircuts; guests of the hotel came in for a second shave before going out for the evening. Downtown merchants left their counters for an hour of gossip with their cronies, and the lordly satraps of the Stockyards descended from their sanguinary thrones to bathe away the stench of the slaughterhouse before returning to marble mansions on Lake Shore Drive. Less affluent visitors settled for a shoeshine and a chance to gaze admiringly at the two hundred and twenty-five silver dollars embedded in the barbershop floor.

The air was a heady mixture of smoke from cheap cubebs,

scented cigarettes, nickel stogies and regal corona coronas, superimposed upon a blend of bourbon and bay rum. Straight razors stropped smoothly against leather or scraped stubbornly along stubbled skin; clippers chewed away at curls and muttonchop whiskers.

Charlie Hogan sat in his appointed place, third chair from the end on the left, getting the customary Saturday-afternoon trim from Al, his regular barber. Everything was proceeding on schedule. Hogan had lit his usual four-o'clock cigar, and Al's voice was droning over the din in ritual recitation of his woes—the long hours, sore feet and other chronic miseries. Like everything else here, even the complaints were part of a serene and established pattern, the traditional approach to soliciting a tip.

Then the door opened and tradition shattered. Al glanced up and his litany suddenly ceased. Conversation in the surrounding chairs faded abruptly to a faint and furtive murmuring. Charlie Hogan stared at the doorway, his jaw slackening so that the cigar started to drop from between his lips. He captured it just in time, as his voice rose stridently over the hush.

"Crissie—what the hell are you doing here?"

She gave him a smile calculated to melt marble, though it had little effect on the stony countenances around her and none whatsoever on Hogan's flinty gaze. *A female—here—in a barbershop?*

"I had to talk to you," Crystal said.

Hogan reddened, conscious of the stares openly upon him and all too aware of the unexpressed thought behind them. *Brazen little baggage. Never knew old Charlie went in for that sort of thing. Wonder what she's up to—do you think he's got her in trouble?*

Hogan fumbled in his pocket, fished out a fifty-cent piece

and handed it to Al as he rose hastily from the chair. He hurried forward, doing his best to ignore encircling eyes and the unspoken implication behind them. Grasping Crystal's arm, he led her to the door.

"Come on, let's get out of here," he muttered.

Still smiling, Crystal allowed herself to be guided into the lobby. Once the barbershop door closed behind them, Hogan released his grip with the alacrity of a man who finds himself clutching a rattlesnake.

"Now, what's the big idea? I told you yesterday—"

"I know." Crystal nodded calmly. "Never darken my doorway again, or words to that effect. Well, this isn't your doorway, is it?"

"No, it's not my doorway you darkened. All you just did was blacken my reputation." Hogan punctuated his reply with furious puffs of cigar smoke. "Haven't you done enough already? Coming to me with that libelous yarn about Carrie Watson's cathouse?"

"But it wasn't libelous. You know it's all true."

"Sure. But if I printed it we'd be sued for libel by everyone you named. Running that story would cost me my job."

"And not running it cost me mine."

"Look, Crissie, maybe I was just blowing off steam. I had to do something to knock a little sense into you." Hogan avoided her gaze. "Matter of fact, I intended to call you tomorrow—"

"And give me my job back?"

"Well—"

Crystal gestured toward a settee in the corner of the lobby. "Can't we sit down?"

Hogan nodded as he followed Crystal to the indicated spot and seated himself beside her. "Now let's get one thing settled," he said. "I'm taking you back, but you're on probation."

"What does that mean?"

"It means there'll be no more monkeyshines. You take regular assignments and follow orders."

"And lose the chance of a lifetime?"

Hogan glanced at her warily. "What are you talking about?"

"Headlines." Crystal's voice was soft, but she spoke with a deliberate emphasis that seemed to capitalize each word. "A Secret Castle In The Heart Of Chicago. Mysterious Disappearance Of A Beautiful Young Girl. Gigantic Insurance Swindle. Prominent Physician Implicated–"

Hogan grimaced. "You're off your chump!"

"That's what I thought, at first." Crystal opened her bag and pulled out a notebook. "But I've been looking up facts and figures. Just listen to this."

He grimaced again, but he listened–listened incredulously. When Crystal concluded, his nod was thoughtful.

"Sounds as if there just might be something in it. Suppose I put a man on Monday–"

"To do what? Go out and ask G. Gordon Gregg if he's perpetrating fraud?" Crystal shook her head. "You won't get anywhere just asking questions."

"Then what do you propose?"

She told him then, and he exploded.

"I might have known! All this hanky-panky just to help get Jim's job back. That's the real reason, isn't it?" Hogan's cigar gestured accusingly. "Well, it won't wash. I'm not going to let you bamboozle me again."

Crystal shrugged. "If I can bring you enough evidence, enough proof to give you an exclusive and make it stick?" She hesitated a moment, letting her words sink in. "Unless, of course, you want me to peddle it over at the *Tribune* instead."

Hogan gestured hastily with the cigar. "That won't be necessary."

"Then you're agreed?"

"Go ahead." Hogan took a deep breath as they rose. "Crissie—"

"Yes?"

"Promise me one thing. Watch your step." His eyes probed her face, but she didn't seem to notice.

"Don't worry. I know what to do."

The hardest part, of course, was facing Jim that evening.

Such a lovely, balmy summer evening it was, too: the lights of the Fair had never been brighter.

"You're in a rare mood," Jim said as they sipped their demitasses at the marble-topped table outside Old Vienna's café.

Crystal nodded. "Things are looking up," she said.

"But aren't you going to tell me what you did this afternoon? Did you see Mr. Hogan? Did he give you your job back—is that it?"

Crystal smiled at him across the table. "I've got a new job."

"What is it?"

"I can't tell you yet; it's a secret."

Jim frowned. "Meaning I wouldn't approve. Look, if this is another one of your wild ideas—"

"Please, don't ask any more questions now. I'll tell you as soon as I can, I promise."

Crystal rose, putting her hand on his arm. "And speaking of promises, didn't you say you'd take me to the Moorish Palace?"

"Yes, I did." Jim stood up and started along the Midway. "Look, at least you can let me know when you'll be working."

"I expect to start on Monday," Crystal said. "Now come along, darling. I want to get a look at that Chamber of Horrors everybody's talking about."

15

As Crystal stood waiting, she was conscious of the stares. The pharmacy was almost deserted at this early-morning hour, and the clerks behind the counter eyed her with idle curiosity. At least, she hoped that was what it was—a pair of youngsters scarcely out of their teens looking at a girl. Perfectly normal, she told herself.

Unless, of course, they had recognized her. But that was impossible. She'd been here only once before, and then she was wearing a veil. It was absolutely out of the question that either one of them would remember her.

Still, she was grateful when Mr. Hickey came bustling back from his trip to the rear of the store. "Come with me, Miss Wilson." She nodded, smiling, then sobered. For he was staring at her over his spectacles. Did he recognize her too? Nonsense: the man was obviously nearsighted; he peered at everything. Better get rid of such ideas quickly, she told herself firmly as Hickey led her to the office beyond the dispensary and gestured to her to enter.

Gregg, rising from behind his desk, was looking her full in the face. There was no idle curiosity in those deep dark eyes, no myopic effort to focus. The doctor's stare was intent and somehow intimate. In his presence, it was hard to remember that the man was what she knew him to be. Or had he glimpsed the face beneath the veil; did he recall it and know her now?

If so, it was too late to turn back. Crystal found the smile and the words.

"Uncle Gordon!"

"My dear young lady, how good of you to come."

The smile was warm, the voice was soothing and the touch of his hand reassuring as he led her to a chair. "Do sit down, Miss Wilson."

"Crystal," she corrected.

"As you wish." Gregg seated himself at the desk, swivelling his chair around to face her. "Frankly, I had no idea . . . I expected to see a child."

"I'm afraid I didn't make myself clear over the telephone," Crystal said. "It came as such a shock when you told me of Aunt Millie's death."

"Poor, dear Millicent." Gregg sighed. "So many months ago and you didn't know. Of course, she'd been out of touch with the family for all these years. I scarcely realized myself that there were still any relatives surviving."

"Just Mama and I," Crystal said. "And Mama's not a great one for writing. But she did send a letter to Aunt Millie in July to tell her I'd be coming."

Gregg shook his head. "I never received it."

"She wrote to the Sunnyside Avenue address," Crystal said.

"That explains it." Gregg nodded solemnly. "The whole house went in the fire, you know."

"How dreadful!"

Gregg sighed. "One has to accept what Providence decrees," he said. "What's done is done, and we must learn to face what will be. And now, my dear, let's talk of pleasanter things. How long do you intend to be in town?"

"Well, as I told you when I called from the depot, I came to see the Fair. And then I was supposed to talk to Aunt Millie about the investment."

"What investment?"

Crystal frowned. "I keep forgetting you never got the letter. She explained it all there. You see, after Papa passed away, his partner sold the store. It was one of the biggest dry-goods stores in San Francisco, but he's an old man without any family, and he didn't see any reason to keep on working. So he sold out and Mama put our share of the money in the bank. Our lawyer keeps telling her we can do better with it than just drawing interest, and she thought she'd ask Aunt Millie for advice before planning anything. But now . . ." Crystal's voice trailed off.

Gregg nodded, tugging at his moustache. "First things first," he said. "I presume you have your luggage?"

"I checked it into the baggage room at the LaSalle Street Station. Of course I thought I'd be staying with Aunt Millie, so I hadn't made hotel reservations."

"That won't be necessary." Gregg rose. "You'll be my guest."

"Here? Oh, but I couldn't impose."

"Impose? This place was built with twenty rooms to accommodate visitors. And the Fair is within walking distance. I'll call down to the station and have your things sent out this afternoon. Come along now and let me make you comfortable."

Crystal came along—through the pharmacy, out into the street and around the corner to Wallace, where a side entrance led to the second story and its corridor lined with identical doors distinguished by metal numerals. Number 3 was a pleasantly furnished little room with private bath and a view of the street.

But she was not comfortable there—not even after the van delivered the bags she had so carefully packed and left at the baggage counter of the station before coming here this morning. Nor was she really comfortable when Gregg knocked on her door shortly after noon, although she greeted him with a ready smile.

"All settled in?" He glanced past her toward the open closet, nodding approval. "I see you're unpacked. And it's time for lunch. You'll join me, of course."

He'd changed clothing, Crystal noted; now he was wearing a bowler, a gray weskit and a tattersall vest.

She suppressed her surprise. "Where are we going?"

"I thought we'd try Washington Park. There's a rather good restaurant at the pavilion there, and you might enjoy the races."

It was obvious that Gregg enjoyed the track. Crystal still found herself unable to relax, even though the meal was excellent. Tension dulled the taste buds, and she was conscious of Gregg's ceaseless scrutiny as he asked the seemingly innocent questions about her background, about her home, about her mother. After all, Mama was poor, dear Millicent's sister.

All Crystal had to go on was Millie Gregg's obituary,

taken from news accounts of the fire. Fortunately, it seemed Gregg had known nothing about the California branch of the family, and she found herself relaxing a trifle as she described her life as the daughter of a wealthy dry-goods merchant; actually, it wasn't too difficult, because she had really spent her childhood in San Francisco. Of course, Daddy was only a minister, and her personal knowledge of Nob Hill was hearsay; still, it seemed to satisfy Gregg. Satisfy, and intrigue him.

It was the bit about the investment that interested him, no doubt of that. He'd risen to the bait just as she'd hoped.

After luncheon, they went to their place in the grandstand. Reserved seats, no less, and he sent out for champagne. "To celebrate the occasion," he explained. "It isn't every day one is fortunate enough to meet a long-lost relative."

Apparently Gregg had indulged in previous celebrations, for the waiter who served them knew him by name. So did the flashily dressed gentleman with whom he put down his bets for the races. No question about it, he was very much at home here, and when they promenaded during the intervals, a number of people smiled and nodded at him in greeting.

"You're quite a celebrity," Crystal said.

"Nonsense." But there was unmistakable pleasure in his response. "Just a local businessman; they know me from the pharmacy."

"Do you come here often?"

Gregg shrugged. "Recently, yes. I find it relaxing. Oddly enough, I frequently recommend such visits to my patients. Fresh air, sunshine, a chance to stretch one's legs. Nothing like innocent recreation to clear the mind of care." He glanced toward the boxes. "And it's an excellent opportunity to observe one's fellowman. Look, my dear, if I'm not mistaken, that broad-shouldered gentleman over there is Gentleman Jim Corbett."

Crystal followed his gaze and nodded. The world's heavyweight champion was surrounded by admirers, including several handsome if flamboyantly gowned young ladies who she suspected might have taken a few hours' respite from the chatter of Carrie Watson's parrot. Her suspicions seemed confirmed when one of them caught Gregg's eye and waved.

He turned away quickly, and she pretended not to have noticed the gestured greeting. "Truly the Sport of Kings," he murmured. "But we'd best get back to our seats. The fifth race is about to begin."

Gregg bet on every race, Crystal noted, and his wagers were lavish—never less than ten and sometimes as high as fifty dollars. Unfortunately, his losses were lavish too. On the sixth race, however, his horse came in, and the bookie bestowed a bundle of greenbacks that more than compensated for his previous losses.

Gregg beamed at her. "You bring me luck." He counted the money carefully, then passed it back to the waiting man. "Samantha in the seventh, to win," he said. "Four to one, isn't she?"

The bookie frowned. "All of it?"

"On the nose." Gregg fingered his moustache. "Fortune taken at the tide, as the Bard says."

Crystal shielded her eyes against the sun as the horses came to the starting gate. "Which is yours?" she murmured.

"Samantha? The roan, with the jockey in yellow. Number One, an auspicious number." He leaned forward. "They're off!"

Together they craned down at the speeding shimmer as it moved around the track. Despite herself, Crystal found her excitement rising. "Come on, Samantha, come on, Number One!"

But then it was over, and Number One proved to be Number Four.

"Maybe I'm not so lucky for you after all," Crystal sighed.

Gregg made a gesture of dismissal. "What's a few dollars more or less?" He grasped Crystal's arm. "Time to go now."

He led her out to the carriage rank and hailed a hack.

"Comfortable?" he asked, settled beside her as they clattered past the exit gate.

She nodded quickly, but averted her gaze. For she was far from feeling at ease yet.

"Sorry we couldn't stay longer," Gregg was saying. "But duty calls."

"I understand."

Gregg pulled out his watch and snapped it open. "After four," he said. "I've got to get back for the interview."

"Interview?"

He nodded, slipping the watch back into his vest pocket. "I've an appointment to see someone from Frobisher's. It's an employment agency downtown. For several weeks now I'm without a secretary, and the way work is piling up—"

"But Uncle Gordon, I'm a secretary."

"You?"

Crystal nodded quickly. "Didn't I tell you? I graduated from business college last year." She turned to face him now. "Why don't you let me have the job?"

"I couldn't do that. You're a guest."

"Why not? I'll be staying here anyway, and I should do something to repay you for your kindness. At least let me help you in the office."

The dark eyes were thoughtful. "Do you typewrite, take dictation?"

"Of course. Please, give me a chance to show you what I can do."

Gregg fingered his moustache. "Perhaps it would solve the problem."

"Say you'll let me." Crystal squeezed his arm. "Why don't I start Monday?"

"But you planned to visit the Fair."

"There's plenty of time for that. And since we're so close by, I can always go over in the evenings, after work. It's a perfect arrangement for both of us."

"Perhaps so." Gregg smiled as he spoke. "Maybe I was right after all when I said you brought me luck."

"Then it's settled, I can have the job?"

"Yes."

"Oh, thank you, thank you."

Crystal snuggled back in her seat. For the first time that day, she felt really comfortable.

16

COMFORT, Crystal discovered, is not necessarily a constant companion. Everything was fine during dinner at a nearby restaurant that evening; but later, when he left her at the Wallace Avenue side entrance and she walked alone to her room on the second floor, all her doubts returned.

Playacting with Gregg had been easy enough; she'd thought everything out, rehearsed herself perfectly. But conversation had ended now, and she had no other resource to combat the realization of her true situation and all it implied. It was one thing to enjoy the triumph of a successful masquerade, but Gregg was playing a game too.

Crystal shook her head. If only she could talk to Jim! But he mustn't know where she was, or why. Nobody knew, except for Charlie Hogan. Actually, he was the only one she could rely on for any help now. Jim wouldn't understand; he'd just be angry. Charlie Hogan got angry too, but then he went ahead and did something about it. He was probably upset with her right now because she hadn't called him to report, but she intended to as soon as she had the opportunity. No chance of reaching him tonight; it was too late. All she could do now was lock her door.

Footsteps sounded in the hall. She strained against the door as they approached and passed. Of course, there were other guests in these rooms, visitors to the Fair. Better get accustomed to the sounds.

But later, lying in bed in the darkness, she found herself listening again, listening to something far worse than any sound: the silence. It was dawn before she slept, and then her slumber was fitful and brief. All too soon the hour came when she had to arise and face the morning.

But comfort was beside her then. Comfort, it seemed, was willing to share the sunlight, and she learned its habits well during the days that followed.

To her relief, Gregg's schedule seemed a simple one; in the morning he devoted himself to dictation, while the afternoons were given over to his medical practice. In that she had no part, for she was too busy typing up the work he'd given her: letters to drug-supply houses, to business firms in the East. All very legitimate correspondence, orders and inquiries. Of course, he handled the incoming mail himself and he didn't show her everything he received. There were personal items he left unopened in her presence—items that he filed away in his desk under lock and key. No way of discovering the content of these missives, any more than she could eavesdrop on his private consultations in the office upstairs.

Meanwhile, the important thing was to fulfill her duties to Gregg's satisfaction, and this seemed to be simple enough. Their working hours together passed quickly, and in the evenings they usually dined together down the street.

In some respects, the arrangement suited her; she had an opportunity to cultivate their acquaintanceship. But that was all it was: merely a superficial relationship between uncle and niece. True, Gregg's castle was hardly an ordinary dwelling; within a few days Crystal had been introduced to the secret staircase behind the second-story door numbered 17. But there was no reason to doubt his explanation of a private entrance and exit to the apartment above. As for the apartment itself, it yielded no secrets to her casual inspection, and since she was never alone in it there was no opportunity to investigate further. She knew there was a locked cabinet in the bedroom, but it was merely a handsome piece of furniture; preposterous to imagine a corpse concealed inside. After a time she learned of a parallel flight of stairs ascending from the first level directly to the private office adjoining the apartment, but this was scarcely mysterious in itself, since patients were frequently conducted there by this route. The private office, too, had its enigmas: the niche behind the anatomy chart, for example, and the locked files. But any practicing physician would protect his case histories and his cash in this fashion. Crystal realized the castle also had a cellar, though she didn't know how one reached it and had never seen Gregg descend there—there would be no need yet for attending to the heating. All she knew was that there were portions of the castle that remained inaccessible, portions she found no way to explore.

Any more than she could fully explore what lay behind Gregg's polite and friendly facade. During the time they spent together when dining at the end of the day she learned

a number of things about Uncle Gordon. He had been born and educated in the East, he was an amateur musician and a connoisseur of food and wine, his wardrobe was extensive and expensive, he seemed more than a little vain of his personal appearance. But these were hardly attributes to excite suspicion.

His manner of speech seemed to vary with his mood; sometimes he was pompously precise, particularly in his dictation of letters and his conversation with drug salesmen and patients, yet when he was alone with her he spoke casually and wasn't above using the slang of the day. Again, this was normal enough for a medical man who separated his professional image from his private personality. If he was addicted to the racetrack, he shared this interest with thousands of other respectable citizens. As for his nocturnal visits to the District, Crystal had only to remember the list of civic leaders and dignitaries with similar tastes; it wasn't an interest in ornithology that caused them to seek out Carrie Watson's parrot.

Finally Crystal decided the best she could do was to find alternative routes. Casually, she cultivated Mr. Hickey. When he came into the downstairs office while Gregg was upstairs, she made a point of being friendly, asking innocent questions. In return, she got innocent answers. Hickey was a licensed pharmacist; he made up most of the routine prescriptions for both patients and customers, and spent much of his time in the dispensary with mortar and pestle when he wasn't busy supervising the activities up front. He'd been hired by Gregg when the place opened, but there was no personal tie between them, and no hint of intimacy. The little bespectacled man seemed perfectly content to compound his nostrums without question, flattered by Gregg's delegation of authority in running the drugstore.

He asked no questions of his distinguished employer and could answer none. The two young clerks, Dan and Perry, were far more interested in the female customers than in the business itself. Crystal tried to sound them out, but they obviously knew nothing of what went on behind the scenes and cared less. To them Dr. Gregg was merely a shadowy figure who moved in a distant world known to them only through the pages of the *Police Gazette*—a world peopled by such awesome celebrities as Sousa and the mighty Sandow. They kept no track of his comings and goings, and for all they knew he might dine nightly with Diamond Jim Brady.

To add to her growing discomfort, Crystal found no way of contacting Jim until she'd been at the castle for almost a week. Twice she'd called from the office, during the afternoon when Gregg was with patients upstairs, and twice there had been no answer. It was impossible to get away in the evenings. She cautiously suggested to him that she wanted to visit the Fair, but he put her off.

"I wouldn't dream of letting you go by yourself—not at night," he told her. "Be patient. I'll take you this weekend, I promise."

Which meant that she couldn't count on her freedom even then. Finally, late Friday afternoon, she reached Jim at his boardinghouse on Harper Avenue.

"Crystal! Where the devil have you been?"

"Now, don't get excited."

"I've been going out of my mind. I called you at the rooming house and they told me you moved out last Monday with no forwarding address. I phoned the paper and Mr. Hogan said you were no longer employed."

"Please, listen to me. I couldn't get hold of you earlier."

"Where are you?"

"At work. I told you I was getting a new job."

"What kind of a job?"

"I can't talk about it now. Wait until I see you."

"Tomorrow?"

"No. Maybe next weekend."

"Next weekend?"

"Jim, I'm sorry."

"Sorry? Is that all you can say?" The angry voice modulated with sudden concern. "Look, are you sure you're all right?"

"Of course I am. Everything's fine. If you'll just be patient and give me a little time, I can explain."

"You'd better explain right now." The anger was back. "You're up to something again, aren't you?"

"I told you I couldn't talk now."

"You can't talk now and you can't see me this weekend. Maybe you don't want to see me at all."

"That's not true. I'll call you next Wednesday, I promise."

"Crystal, for the last time—"

"Wednesday."

She put the phone down then, and with it her last vestige of security. It was a rotten trick, she knew, but there was nothing else she could do. And in a few days now, everything would be straightened out—just as soon as she found what she was looking for. If there was anything to find.

But the days passed without discovery or development. True to his word, Gregg took her to the Fair on Saturday and again on Sunday. They inspected the panoramas of the Bernese Alps and the volcano of Kilauea, dined at the Chinese Tea House and the Clambake, toured the Indian Bazaar and the other Midway exhibits to which a proper uncle might escort an impressionable niece. The crowds jostled their way toward the amusement area, but Uncle Gordon found it more educational to tour the Horticulture

Building and admire the orchids. On Sunday evening they stayed for the fireworks, but there were no added illuminations for her; she made no progress in her quest.

One thing, and only one, gave Crystal a measure of encouragement. Gregg was beginning to talk about poor, dear Mama.

"Have you heard from her?" he inquired, as they left the grounds that evening and sought a hack.

Crystal shook her head. "It's too early. I didn't write until Tuesday and she probably hasn't even received my letter yet. But she'll be so happy when she learns I'm working for you."

"I'm worried about her." Gregg frowned. "You say she's all alone, no one else left to look after her?"

"There's Mr. Pilchrist."

"Who's he?"

"The lawyer. I told you about him."

"Ah, yes. The lawyer." In the shadows of the moving hack, Gregg's hand brushed the waxed tips of his moustache. "We'll have to talk about that, won't we? This matter of savings and possible investments. Your mother's future must be properly provided for. Your future, too. I'm very busy right now, but I intend to give the matter some thought."

"There's no need to concern yourself."

"I can't help it." They left the hack before the Wallace Avenue entrance to the upstairs lodgings. "I must say you've made a very good impression on me, my dear. For someone who has never held a secretarial position before you're making a remarkable adjustment. But you certainly don't intend to waste the rest of your life on a business career."

"It's very interesting, Uncle Gordon."

"So are the exhibits at the Fair. Yet they're nothing compared with the real thing. Wouldn't you like to travel, see

the actual places instead of the make-believe? Haven't you ever wanted to visit the Pyramids, the Taj Mahal, the cathedral of Notre Dame? The world is so wide, so full of pleasures, and now is the time to taste them all, while you're still young."

"I'm afraid those things are a little rich for my blood."

"Nothing is impossible. Nothing." Gregg gave her a sidelong glance. "How much did you say your dear mother has available from the sale of the business?"

"I really don't know. It's my impression there's enough to keep her comfortably."

"Properly handled, her capital could bring her far more than mere comfort. And far more than that for you, too. As you grow older, you'll learn not to settle for anything less than luxury." Gregg led her to the door and opened it. "But we'll discuss this further another time."

They said good night then, and she went up the stairs alone. In her room, Crystal prepared for bed, her thoughts preoccupied with recollection. Gregg had expressed interest in her mother's money, but nothing more. Still, the week with him hadn't been a total loss. She'd carried it off as she intended, and as long as he believed there was money in the family he'd be patient with her.

But what if she were wrong? What if there was no real secret to learn; suppose Gregg was just an ordinary petty swindler who liked the ladies, who had his little fling and shrugged it off, went on his merry way to other conquests and consoled himself in the interim at Carrie Watson's?

No, something told her there had to be more than that. Something about his eyes—those deep, dark eyes, staring at her with a suggestion of potential power. There was a secret here, a secret in those eyes, in this place.

For a brief period during the next few days, Crystal

thought she knew a way to find it. The key had been right there, right under her nose, all this time. Sometimes literally under her nose, huddled on all fours in the outer hallway, scrubbing the corridor floor with dogged diligence. Maggie, the upstairs maid, the cleaning woman, the sweeper, the duster, the changer of bed linen in all the rented rooms.

It wasn't difficult to strike up a conversation with Maggie; the day's drudgery made her welcome an opportunity for small talk. But small talk was all she had to offer. Yes, there was work aplenty, and no wonder, what with the way Misther Gregg rented to overnighters—it was a land-office business he did here, and no mistake. Sure and a body did get tuckered out, always running afther thim all, fetching extry pillows and filling up the water pitchers, to say nothing of emptying the crockery under the beds, if the young lady took her meaning.

Crystal took her meaning, and demanded more. Cautiously, she inquired about upstairs.

"One thing I'll say for him, the Misther kapes it nate," she said. "It's little enough I have to bother with in his quarters. A bit of dusting is all he wants; the rest he tends to."

"You've never done any real housecleaning, then?"

"Sure and whin would I be afther doing it, with so much on me hands roight here? You've seen me hours, Miss—up at six, and still at it long past dark. Why, it's nigh bedtime before I'm off to a bit o' supper with the folks on Archer Avenue."

To her surprise, Crystal discovered that Maggie had come to work here only the week before her own arrival. And on Wednesday she was gone again—presumably back on Archer Avenue for good. Another face had taken over her place and duties, answering to the name of Bridget in as broad a brogue, but answering to little else.

She asked Gregg about it that morning and he shrugged. "I'm used to it," he said. "They come and go every few weeks. I know the work is hard, but I pay good wages. Oh well, that's the Irish for you: give them a few dollars and they're off to rush the growler at the nearest saloon. Not that I've any prejudices, mind you, but that's the way it goes, and one must make the best of it. You'll notice I don't give any of them any real responsibilities. I handle all the room rentals myself. Which reminds me, we'll have to total the receipts from upstairs today. It's the end of the month, and I want to keep the records up to date."

"But you've already given me those letters to transcribe."

"Month's end is our busy time. Bills to go out to patients." Gregg smiled at her. "Perhaps you'll be willing to work on the receipts for me this evening."

"I was hoping I might be able to get away for a few hours."

"To the Fair again?" Gregg shook his head. "It's not advisable for you to travel alone after dark. There's a pretty rough element hanging around the Midway. They tell me the police are on the lookout for rowdies, but no sense taking risks." He sobered. "Don't be cross with me, Crystal. We can go again this weekend."

And so she didn't get a chance to call Jim after all. Instead, after dinner, she sat in the downstairs office and totaled rent receipts. There were a great many of them—a surprising number for just a single month; but then, Gregg had so many rooms available. Besides, she supposed a constant turnover was only natural. The guests stayed just long enough to visit the Fair and see the sights—a few days at most. Crystal noted that the majority of them were female. Women probably preferred to take lodgings close to the Fair rather than travel all the way from downtown hotels, where the prices were so high to begin with. Or was that the reason?

Crystal shook her head, fighting a wave of weariness. The reason didn't matter. Why not admit the truth? She'd failed. Ten days of effort, and there was nothing to show for it, nothing at all. If anything, she was in a worse situation than she had been when she started. In a way, it was ironic. She had come here intending to spy on Gregg and instead he had her under his own constant surveillance. She had intended to trap him, but it was she who was trapped now: sitting here like a prisoner, afraid even to pick up the phone and call Jim lest Gregg take it into his head to come downstairs and walk in on her.

What would Jim think if she didn't call? What was he thinking now? She'd have to tell him the truth; there was no other way. And what about Charlie Hogan, waiting for the word, for the story she'd promised him?

It had all seemed so simple, so easy—coming here, gaining Gregg's confidence, keeping her eyes and ears open until he made a slip and she could lay her hands on the evidence to confirm her suspicions. But it wasn't working out. She could sit here and suspect until the cows came home and still nothing would come of it.

Why sit here and stew about it? Suppose Gregg did discover her identity: nothing would be hurt but her pride. But every moment that she delayed she was hurting Jim. He deserved to know the truth; she owed him that. Come what might, she had to call him—call him right now.

Crystal reached for the telephone. But before she could pick it up, the night bell of the pharmacy jangled. It must have been an emergency. The store was closed and darkened; no one would come here at this hour unless his errand was urgent.

The bell jangled again. Automatically, Crystal rose and made her way down the hall, into the dim aisle of the shop. The bell echoed insistently as she moved to the front door; its shade was drawn, but she could see the silhouetted figure behind it, waiting for her approach.

The bell's harsh clangor mingled with the sound of the sliding bolt as Crystal unlocked the door. Then she opened it and admitted the man from the street.

17

HE SWAYED, and she caught a gust of liquor on his breath.

"Where's Doc?" The man peered past her, mumbling, "Got to see Doc."

"Here I am."

Crystal started at the sound of the voice directly behind her. She turned to meet Gregg's nod as he moved up beside her, staring at the man, and she glimpsed the momentary startlement in his eyes.

"Well," he said. "This is a surprise."

The man's chuckle was harsh. "I'll bet it is."

"But a pleasant one." Gregg smiled, then glanced at Crystal quickly. "It's all right," he said. "Thaddeus is an old friend."

"Old and thirsty." The man chuckled again. "And that's the truth."

Gregg's hand dipped into his pocket. "If this will be of any help . . ."

"Not what I had in mind," the man muttered. "Old friends should drink together."

"Then we'll go upstairs." He turned to confront Crystal. "Almost finished? Good; you can close up when you're done. I'll go over the totals in the morning." He moved back down the aisle. "Come along, Thad."

Crystal bolted the door again, then glanced over her shoulder as Gregg and the stranger moved down the aisle past the dispensary. In the faint light fanning forth from the office doorway beyond, she was able to see Thaddeus clearly. He was a hulking, broad-shouldered man with a shambling gait, wearing a shabby teamster's jacket and shapeless corduroy trousers. The contrast between this figure and the immaculately appointed Gregg was almost grotesque, but not nearly as grotesque as Gregg's reaction. He had been startled, she realized, and for a moment she had sensed more than mere surprise.

Gregg was afraid of this man.

Slowly Crystal walked down the aisle, watching the two men moving into the hall that angled off at the end of the office area. She half-expected Gregg to halt before the door that led up to the second floor; instead he passed by and stopped before a second paneled door farther down the corridor. Strange, she'd seen that door a dozen times and never given it another thought; if she'd noticed it at all, her assumption had dismissed it as a broom closet.

But Gregg's key was in the lock, the door was opening and his hand went out to the gas jet mounted on the wall inside. As the light flared, she saw the stairs. Then the two men moved through the doorway and started to ascend as the paneled surface swung shut behind them.

Crystal frowned. Another staircase—to where? And who was this drunken stranger that Gregg should fear him? The answer to these questions lay behind the door. Useless to think of following them; Gregg wouldn't leave anything unlocked.

But he had. She'd seen them going up the steps before it shut. Surprise and fear had overruled precaution. Unless, of course, the door locked automatically when closed from the inside.

There was only one way to find out. Slowly, she moved along the hall, reached for the knob, turned it. The door swung open.

Crystal stared upward at the steep flight slanting into the gloom beyond the gas jet's rays. The two men had disappeared above; the staircase was silent, deserted. She began to ascend, one step at a time, halting to make sure that no sound disturbed the stillness, but she didn't stop completely until she reached the topmost stair, which ended in abrupt confrontation with the door set in the passage's end above.

It was from beneath the door that a sliver of light shimmered over the steps. And it was from behind the door that she could hear the murmur of voices.

Suddenly, she realized where they were—in the office adjoining the apartment. But how could it be possible? She'd never noticed another door on that wall.

Well, You were looking for secret passageways; now you've found one. Crystal frowned again. *Stop talking to yourself. Listen to the voices.*

Gregg's voice. "Say when."

And Thad's chuckle. "That'll do for now. Just leave the bottle where it's handy."

Crystal heard the creak of a chair. Evidently Thad was making himself comfortable. "Ah, that's better. Nice place you got here, Doc."

"I'm glad you approve. But would you mind telling me just how you happened to find it?"

"Sure thing. I spotted you at the races the other day."

"Washington Park?"

"That's right. I was going to sing out, but then I said to myself, No, not in front of the young lady."

"Very considerate of you."

"Still the same old skirt chaser, eh, Doc?"

"Nothing of the sort. The girl's my niece, from San Francisco. I hired her as a secretary."

"Now, don't go getting up on your high horse; I was only asking."

There was an edge of irritation in Gregg's voice. "And so am I. You say you saw me at the track. Then what?"

"Then I asked around. Pointed you out to one of the hokey-pokey vendors. He knew you right off, told me about this place. You're quite a celebrity, Doc." Another chuckle. "So here I am."

"Yes, here you are." The irritation was open now. "What do you want?"

"Easy, now. Is that any way to talk to an old friend? Someone who goes all the way back to the Elmira days? Hell, I knew you when your name was still—"

"Never mind!" Gregg spoke quickly, but Thad wasn't silenced.

"Easy for you to say, isn't it? Now that you're such a swell, living on the fat of the land. G. Gordon Gregg, M.D., what a laugh, you with just one year in medical college!"

"That's enough!"

"Enough for you, perhaps, but not for yours truly. I was

the one who did all the dirty work, and don't you ever forget it. I dug those stiffs up from the marble orchard as fast as they were planted; I peddled them to the dissection lab for you while you sat back proper as you please and pocketed the cash."

"What are you complaining about? You'd never have been able to pull off those jobs if I hadn't planned them. And you got your cut."

"Some planning, those fake permits you forged for me to show the dean when I brought in a specimen. I might of known they'd find out it was a put-up job."

"You forget that I took the blame for that, even though I knew they'd expel me."

"I forget nothing. Sure, you got expelled. That was the deal: you got out of town and they hushed the whole thing up because they didn't want any part of a mess that had to do with one of their own students. But who stood trial for the grave-robbing charges? Who got put away for five goddam years in state prison?"

"You were paid for that, too. All the money I had, and then some."

"Not all. You think I don't know what you were up to with that fiancée of yours and her insurance policy? Mighty convenient of her to have an accident just about then. Leaky gas jet . . ."

"You don't know what you're talking about." Gregg's voice rose to an angry shout, then softened. "Look, it can't be helped now. Here, have another drink."

"Sure."

Crystal tensed, listening to the gurgle, the clinking sound. And then, again, Thad's voice.

"That's the ticket, isn't it, Doc? Pay me off with a shot of whiskey. Well, that's not what I had in mind when I came here."

"I offered you money."

"You won't buy me off with a handout, either."

"Then what do you want?"

"The same deal we had in the old days. Fifty-fifty. Of this and everything."

Surprisingly, it was Gregg who chuckled now. "I went in to hock up to my ears to build this place. Would you like fifty percent of my debts?"

"Don't con me." Thad's voice was harsh. "How long has it been since the last time we saw each other, six, seven years? I'm not the same chump you roped into stir with a swindle and a phony pitch. I learned a lot while I was inside, and I learned more after I come out, even if I was on my uppers most of the time. All this poor-mouth talk of yours—"

"It's the truth, so help me."

"You don't need any help. Drugstore doing a land-office business, patent-medicine racket, doctoring on the side, and on top of it all you're renting to folks visiting the Fair. They say you're coining money."

"You're willing to believe everything you hear? Come on, Thaddeus, if you've learned as much about life as you claim, you know better than to put your trust in idle gossip."

"Damned right I do. Which is why I didn't come around until I had a chance to do a little studying on my own."

"Studying?"

"You'd be surprised what you can find out from reading old newspapers, Doc. There was a story about you in the files, you and your wife, that is. Must of been a pretty big fire. And from what I read later, must have been a pretty big insurance policy, too. Know what it reminded me of?

That poor, dear fiancée of yours and the leaky gas jet blowing her to kingdom come."

"Shut up!"

"I intend to. Just as soon as we come to terms."

"I'm warning you, you can't blackmail me."

"Matter of opinion." Thad's chuckle sounded. "But I don't expect that'll be necessary. Not as long as you play square. This time I'm not getting the dirty end of the stick, and if you got any ideas about arranging an accident for me, you can forget it. I'm on to all your tricks. Besides, I have a hunch you could use a little help."

"What makes you say that?"

"This castle of yours. You didn't build it just to show off. You got plans."

"Perhaps." Gregg's voice was thoughtful. "But I'd need someone I could trust."

"Then it's settled?"

"Not so fast. I don't like this drinking of yours."

"Don't worry, I'll cut out the boozing. Just give me a chance to get located, clean myself up."

"That's no problem. You can stay in one of the rooms here and start tomorrow."

"Doing what?"

"I'll have to line things up. But there's some carpentry work to begin with."

"Want me to build some boxes?" Thad's chuckle rose. "Sounds just like old times."

"Forget about old times," Gregg said. "We don't need boxes, and we're not dealing with medical schools, either. What I have in mind is far bigger than that. You'll see."

As he spoke, Gregg was rising; Crystal heard the sounds through the door, heard the footsteps. Hastily she edged her way back down the stairs, praying she'd reach the lower level in time.

She made it, closing the bottom door with a sigh of relief, then hurried to the office. Extinguishing the light, she left and went round to the Wallace Avenue entrance outside without a further glimpse of Gregg and his companion.

But in her room, even after she'd undressed and crawled into bed, she could still hear the echo of Gregg's voice. *"You'll see."*

She intended to.

18

"CRAZY! That's what it is, just plain crazy!"

Crystal glanced quickly around the Rathskeller, then turned to Jim, shaking her head. "Please, you don't have to shout."

"It's about time somebody shouted at you. Of all the idiotic stunts I ever heard of, this takes the cake!"

"I told you, there's nothing to worry about." Crystal reached across the table for Jim's hand, but she couldn't touch his scowl. "I'm sorry I couldn't tell you sooner, but I was afraid of just such an outburst as this."

"Don't you think I have a right to be concerned?"

"Of course you do. This is something that concerns us both. You want your job back and I want mine."

"And you think you're going to solve the problem by playing amateur detective?"

"I have solved it! If you'll just calm down and listen to me—"

Jim listened, but none too calmly. And when Crystal concluded, he shook his head.

"I still don't see what you're driving at. You've been there two weeks now and you admit yourself that you haven't found anything." He shrugged. "What if he does have a concealed safe and keeps his files locked? That's normal business procedure. Even Mr. Follansbee does exactly the same thing. There's no proof of Gregg having anything hidden away that would really incriminate him, and if he does, you still can't find a way of getting to it."

"But we needn't bother with getting to it now. We've got Thad."

Jim took a sip of beer. "You say he's been doing carpentry work. What kind?"

"I don't know. But I can hear the banging and pounding all day long, even from where I sit in the office."

"In that case, so can everyone else. He can't be doing anything important."

"Maybe not now. But he has. He and Gregg were together from the beginning. He knows all about him."

"What does he know about you?"

"Only that I'm Gregg's niece and secretary. I see him when he comes in to speak to Gregg during the day. We've never had a chance to talk together."

"Do you think it would do any good if you could talk to him?" Jim frowned. "What do you have in mind? Starting a flirtation—getting him drunk—waiting for him to spill the beans about everything, just like that?"

"Now you're the one who's being idiotic." Crystal shook

her head. At the same time, she reached for the purse resting on the table before her, opened it and removed an envelope. "When I found out Gregg was going to the track this afternoon, I called and arranged to meet you here. But on the way I stopped by to see a friend of Charlie Hogan's, over at the Detective Bureau. He gave me this."

Jim opened the envelope and scanned its contents quickly.

"You see?" Crystal murmured. "He did serve that term for grave robbery he mentioned the other night, but notice what he's been up to since. Armed robbery in Buffalo, wanted for assault in Cleveland, suspicion of—"

"I can read." Jim shrugged impatiently. "Did you tell the police where to find him?"

"Not yet. Not until we can make a deal."

"What sort of a deal?"

"Reducing the charges, in return for telling them everything he knows about G. Gordon Gregg."

"You really think it can work?"

"I'm sure of it." Crystal leaned forward. "I'll find a way of contacting Hogan over the weekend, tell him what's up. He has connections with the department. Let him make the arrangements. Once they pick up Thad, it's all over."

"If he talks."

"Don't worry." Crystal rose, slipping the envelope back into her purse. "He'll talk, all right." She spoke with a conviction that clung to her until she returned to the pharmacy in the late afternoon.

When she entered the office she found Gregg seated at his desk. He glanced at her quizzically.

"Hickey tells me you've been out."

"That's right—I had some shopping to do downtown."

Crystal displayed the box under her arm, congratulating

herself on the foresight that had prompted the last-minute purchase. "I bought a new skirt."

"Good." But he was still staring at her.

Crystal smiled quickly. "And what about you: did you have a good day at the track?"

Gregg's eyes never left her face. "I didn't go. Something came up at the last minute." He sighed softly. "Help is so unreliable nowadays."

There was a hint of veiled accusation in his voice which she thought she had better face. "I hope you—I haven't done anything to displease you."

"Certainly not." He shook his head. "It's that handyman I've had doing odd jobs around here."

"Thad Hoskins?"

"Yes. He decided to quit on me."

"You mean he's left?"

"Without any notice. Just packed up his things and disappeared." Gregg shrugged. "Fortunately, his work was finished."

"Maybe he just took off on a spree." Crystal was talking to herself as much as to Gregg. "He'll probably turn up again on Monday morning."

"I doubt if that's likely." Gregg shook his head slowly. "No, my dear, I'm afraid he's gone for good."

19

ON SUNDAY AFTERNOON, just as he'd promised, Uncle Gordon escorted Crystal to the Fair. The waters of the Basin sparkled under the September sun, but the bulk of the crowd moved along the Midway, seeking its pleasures as though conscious of autumn's imminence. Summer vacations had ended for the young, and their elders must heed the sober summons of fall—the hustle of the city or the harvest of the far-off farms. There was an impatience in the air, an urgency on the part of all to enjoy a final fling.

Crystal sensed the mood and shared it, but she found no enjoyment here.

"Tired, my dear?" Gregg asked, as they emerged from the Indian Bazaar.

"A little."

"Let's rest awhile." He led her to a table outside the French Café. As he ordered drinks, she excused herself and moved inside. She found the public telephone at the rear of the establishment and hastily inserted a nickel.

Jim must have been sitting by the phone, for he answered at the first ring.

"Crystal, where are you?"

"At the Fair."

"He's with you?" There was concern in his voice.

"Yes. I can only talk a minute."

"What did you find out?"

"Nothing."

He sounded troubled. "You mean you haven't seen Thad yet?" Very troubled now.

Crystal hesitated.

"Not yet. But I'll call as soon as I get some word."

"Tomorrow?"

She took a deep breath. "Please don't worry, darling. I'll be in touch as soon as I can." And hung up, cursing her cowardice. But she couldn't tell him the rest—any more than she could call Charlie Hogan and admit her failure.

Crystal turned and started back to the tables outside. She couldn't stall much longer. Tomorrow, Jim had said, and tomorrow it must be. The sooner he knew the truth, the sooner he could make a serious effort to find another job. It wasn't right to keep him dangling with false hopes.

For some reason or other, the idea of facing up to Charlie Hogan was even worse. She'd let him down again, after all her promises, all her hopes. What could she say to him?

Conscience doth make cowards of us all. Daddy liked to quote Shakespeare. And he'd done more than offer her the solace of quotation. She couldn't count the times she had come to him with problems and found solutions. But he was gone now. All she had was—

"Uncle Gordon."

He sat there smiling at her, smiling and waiting. So stiff and dapper, not a hair of his brilliantined pompadour out of place, not a bristle of his waxed moustache disturbed. He set down his glass and beckoned her to a seat beside him.

"Feeling better?"

She nodded, forcing a smile.

"Here, drink this." Crystal raised her glass automatically. He'd ordered wine for himself, a lemonade for her. All quite charming and correct. G. Gordon Gregg, the proper gentleman! "I've been considering your problem," he said.

"Problem?" Crystal controlled herself with an effort, conscious of his smiling scrutiny.

"Remember our little talk the other day? About your mother's financial arrangements?"

"Oh, that."

"Don't dismiss it so lightly. Your future is involved as well as hers."

Crystal's hand tightened around her glass. She'd almost forgotten about the bait so carefully cast to lead and lure, but now he was rising to it at last. She nodded.

"I appreciate that. But as I told you, Mr. Pilchrist—"

"Mr. Pilchrist is a lawyer, not an investment counselor." Fish are greedy creatures; they do not share their prey. "One doesn't need legal advice to place funds in a savings account. And twenty thousand at compound interest brings in an annual income sufficient to live on in straitened circumstances. But what if one isn't satisfied with a life of genteel poverty?"

"Mother isn't in want."

"Of course not. Neither are you. And yet I can't help wishing better things for you both." The smooth voice murmured on—the swindler's voice. How many times had he spoken these words, and to how many people?

Crystal frowned. "Mother is rather conservative."

"An admirable trait. But one which, unfortunately, is seldom found among those who have achieved financial independence." Gregg gestured. "All investment, all speculation involves a gamble. But the successful gambler is the one who knows how to gamble on a sure thing. That's the secret of success."

Crystal shrugged. "Doesn't everyone think he has a sure thing when he invests his money? How can you really be certain?"

"Only through experience." Gregg leaned forward. "And I'm offering my own. Five years ago I was penniless. I had nothing, absolutely nothing. Within a few years, the little I was able to set aside from my income as a pharmacist and physician pyramided into a small fortune. Because I invested in a sure thing—the one thing I had complete and utter confidence in. I invested in myself."

He smiled. The fish was a shark, and a shark has teeth. "You've seen my establishment. You know the volume of business I'm doing there. But that's only the beginning. In a few more weeks the Fair will end, and receipts from room rentals will drop. I'm not worried about this. Because then I'll be free to pursue bigger plans." Gregg's fingertips met the tips of his moustache. "The secret is in the castle."

Crystal stared as he nodded slowly.

"You know me well enough by this time to realize I'm not eccentric. I believe in modern methods, the scientific approach. Haven't you ever asked yourself why I decided to build such an architectural monstrosity?"

"I've wondered about that." Crystal hesitated, choosing her words carefully. "Of course it does attract the eye . . ."

"Exactly. And because of the Fair, people's eyes are being opened, opened to the whole world beyond their doorsteps. I deliberately designed the castle to excite their curiosity. The experiment was successful. And now I intend to go on."

Gregg lifted his glass, his dark eyes staring at her across its rim. "Why stop at a castle? Why not a Taj Mahal on the North Side, a cathedral out on Garfield, a miniature palace downtown?" He drained his glass, lowered it. "Makes sense, doesn't it?"

"Yes," Crystal murmured. And it was true, it did make sense, in a crazy sort of way. For a moment she almost believed it herself, just as he seemed to. Until he spoke.

"I want you to think it over, my dear. If you agree, if you can see the possibilities, then write your mother. Tell her what an opportunity exists here. I'll be happy to help you explain. I have the plans for financing all worked out. We can form a corporation, arrange for you to receive her power of attorney if you like, but we can go over the details later. For now, all I ask is that you keep this in strictest confidence until I can show you the facts and figures. Agreed?"

"Yes, Uncle Gordon."

The mouth beneath the moustache formed. The shark was satisfied for the moment; having swallowed the bait, it would hang on, confident of capturing its prey. There would be no struggle until it felt the hook.

Gregg rose. "We'd better go now. There'll be guests checking out tonight. And I'd like a word with the new maid."

Crystal pushed her chair back from the table. "What happened to Bridget?"

"She gave notice." He smiled resignedly. "I've engaged a replacement. Elsa Krause; she seems a good, solid, dependable sort. Maybe we'll have better luck with the Germans."

Crystal considered the matter that night in her room as she sat before the mirror and brushed her hair. Today had been a reprieve; Gregg's interest would give her additional time, though she doubted she could test his patience for very long.

Footsteps sounded softly along the corridor outside, and somewhere in the distance a door creaked. Probably one of the guests arriving or departing. They came and went, just like the maids, and all the others. The others who had come and gone over the months. Maybe it was their ghosts she heard, haunting the halls. It was easy to doubt in daylight, but not at night. By day one could accept the departure of visitors. When darkness came, they were still here—not visitors, but victims.

Crystal set down the brush and stared at herself in the glass. Was she a victim too? Why not? It was so easy to be blinded, to see only what one wanted to see. All she'd been looking for was an answer to suit her own selfish purposes. She'd turned away her eyes from other things—unpleasant things, things that decent, respectable people don't care to examine.

The spectacle of dying, of death by violence. Eyes bulging, mouth twisted in agony, limbs twitching, blood gushing and spurting. Why think only of the perpetrators of pain? It is the victims one must care about, the victims who must be acknowledged and avenged.

Something thudded overhead. An echo wailed between the walls. Crystal shook her head. So many doors, so many rooms, staircases, passages. First they open, then they swallow and close, hiding their secrets. Absurd, of course. And yet hadn't Gregg said it? He'd given her the answer without knowing it.

The secret is in the castle.

20

Detective sergeant stanley murdoch smelled of cloves and Sen-Sen. His handlebar moustache, like his hair, was the color of ginger. From time to time it twitched in accompaniment with the moving mouth beneath as the Sergeant shifted his chewing tobacco from cheek to cheek. A squat, burly man with a bright, florid face, he sat behind his desk, exuding assurance, as solid and substantial as the cuspidor resting beside his feet.

"I'm sorry, Miss. You should have told me all this when you came and requested Thad Hoskins' record last week. We could have picked him up." The Sergeant stared at Crystal accusingly. "It was your duty to inform us, you know. A man with a known criminal record, wanted by the police."

"But I intended to tell you, just as soon as I had a chance to question him . . ."

"Too late for that now." Sergeant Murdoch drew a bead on the cuspidor, aimed, fired. "Next time, leave the questioning to us."

"There won't be a next time!" Crystal leaned forward, gesturing impatiently. "Don't you understand? He's gone now, just like all the others I told you about."

"So you say." Sergeant Murdoch glanced down at Crystal's penciled notes before him. "But the coroner's report establishes that Millicent Gregg died in a fire. The insurance man you mention spoke to Genevieve Bolton himself. She's in Kansas City, just as Dr. Gregg told you. And if he tells you Thaddeus Hoskins up and quit, what's there to disprove it?"

"But the other secretary, the one who worked for him before Genevieve Bolton: you're forgetting that she disappeared too."

"Alice Porter?" Murdoch shook his head. "It's the same story. He said she left. Again, just your word against his."

"What about Gregg's personal history? I told you what I overheard when he and Hoskins were together. Surely you can check it out."

"We'll make inquiries."

"And if something happens in the meantime?" Crystal's voice broke.

"Now, calm down, Miss Wilson." To judge the movements of Murdoch's mouth, he was finding it difficult to take his own advice. "There's no sign anything is going to happen, and no proof yet that anything has happened."

"All I'm asking is that you see for yourself." Crystal jabbed a finger at the notes she'd placed on Murdoch's desk.

"These staircases and passageways actually exist. That fake room, number seventeen, leads directly up to his apartments. If you'd only investigate, I know you'd find the answer."

"You expect the Department to issue a search warrant on the basis of what you've got here?" Murdoch shook his head. "A man's entitled to build his home any way he wants. No law against that, is there?"

"Then you won't help me?" Crystal's voice faltered.

"I said we'd look into his record." Murdoch rose. "Now, Miss, if you'll excuse me . . ."

Crystal turned away. As she left the office, she heard the telltale *ping* of the cuspidor behind her. What a miserable excuse for a policeman, this contented cow, chewing its cud!

Well, there was nowhere to go now except back to the castle, where Gregg waited. He seemed to accept her excuse about the dental appointment—he could verify it if he liked, because Hogan had set it up for her with a dentist friend downtown. And he seemed to accept her story that she had written a letter to her mother about the investment. She still had time, but it meant nothing now. After Murdoch, she felt as if the last door had closed.

Then, Friday morning, Mr. Hickey came into the office as Gregg was dictating. "Gentleman to see you, Doctor."

Gregg looked up, annoyed. "I've no appointment."

"But he insisted it was important."

"Who is he, what does he want?"

"A Mr. Glass."

"That's right." A figure moved into the office behind Hickey and nodded at Gregg. "I'm from the Building Inspector's office."

Crystal turned, then blinked. That ginger-colored handlebar moustache. Sergeant Murdoch gave her a casual glance which held no hint of recognition. And although he was undisguised, she had to look twice to assure herself that this was the same man she'd spoken to at the Bureau. He seemed to have discarded his air of authority along with his tobacco: there was a slight stoop to his shoulders, a meekness of manner and voice which caught Crystal by surprise.

Gregg was rising. "Yes, Mr. Glass. What can I do for you?"

Murdoch fished a card from his pocket and handed it to Gregg. "Sorry to disturb you, sir. But there seems to have been an oversight." His hand dipped into his pocket again, bringing out a battered, bulky notebook. "According to our records, this construction job was completed without final inspection."

Gregg's eyebrows arched. "My contractor was responsible for plans and permits. I was under the impression he filed the necessary information with your office." He glanced toward the desk. "If I recall correctly, I have a filing receipt here somewhere. I'd be glad to show you—"

"That won't be necessary." Murdoch nodded. "All we need is a routine inspection of the finished job. Just a formality, you understand. If you could spare me a half hour?"

"Now?" Gregg frowned. "I'm rather busy at the moment."

"I understand, sir. If you like, I could come back again this afternoon."

"I'm afraid I'm tied up with my medical appointments."

"Of course." Murdoch was unperturbed. "Tomorrow morning, then."

"Look, you say it's only a formality." Gregg moved forward, lowering his voice to a confidential level as he put his hand on Murdoch's arm. "If there's something to fill out and sign, why not do it now and consider the matter settled? My time is valuable, and I'm sure yours is too. And if it's a question of recompense for your trouble . . ." He broke off with a shrug.

But its significance seemed lost on Murdoch. "No trouble at all, sir." He shook his head. "It's my job." Then, patiently, "Would tomorrow noon be more convenient?"

Gregg's hand dropped from Murdoch's arm. For an instant he turned away, masking and mastering irritation. "Let's get it over with," he said.

"Thank you."

And thank you, Sergeant Murdoch, Crystal told herself. *You're not the fool I took you to be, after all.*

"What do you want me to show you?" Gregg was asking. "The pharmacy here . . ."

"I did some looking around as I came in," Murdoch said. He glanced at the notebook. "Suppose we start with your living quarters upstairs."

"Very well." Gregg moved toward the doorway. "We'll have to go outside for that. The entrance is on Wallace, around the corner."

Crystal bit her lip. What about the staircase leading up from the hallway here? She'd told Murdoch about that; had he forgotten?

As the two men started into the hall, she rose and followed. "Dr. Gregg, will you be needing me?" she called.

Gregg turned, shaking his head. "Not until I'm finished with this."

"I thought I might go up to my room for a few minutes, if you don't mind."

"By all means." Gregg turned away again, just long enough for Crystal to catch Murdoch's eye and gesture quickly in the direction of the two paneled doors at the far end of the corridor.

Murdoch nodded imperceptibly, and Crystal felt the surge of relief. *He remembers . . .*

Then Murdoch was moving forward. "Oh, Doctor, before we go."

"Yes?"

"Those doors at the end of the hall. Where do they lead to?"

"Nowhere."

Nowhere? Crystal tensed. *Please, Sergeant–don't let him get away with it.*

"Might I take a look, sir?"

Gregg sighed. "Of course." He produced the skeleton key from his pocket, unlocked the first door, opened it, stepped aside. "Here we are."

Crystal stared into a tiny square cubicle, cluttered with mops and cleaning utensils.

"A broom closet," Gregg said. "I apologize for its appearance. I've just engaged a new cleaning woman, and I'm afraid tidiness is not one of her virtues."

He moved along, without waiting for a response, and unlocked the second door. It swung open to disclose another cubicle lined with shelves piled high with bottles and cartons. "Pharmaceutical supplies, as you can see. One can't do with too much storage space."

Murdoch nodded, peering at the array for a moment, and then Gregg closed the door and turned the key in the lock. "Some dangerous drugs in there," he murmured. "One must take precautions."

"I understand," Murdoch said. But his swift sidelong glance toward Crystal said he didn't understand. Nor did she.

What had become of the staircase?

All Crystal could do was turn and follow the two men out through the pharmacy, around to the Wallace Avenue entrance which led to the second floor. And there she had to leave them when she came to her room, pretending to fumble with her key in the lock as they continued down the hall to the far end, where another door opened upon a staircase up to the apartment above. She knew of the existence of that staircase; knew also that Gregg seldom if ever used it. He came and went in secret, by the other routes. *Routes that didn't exist.*

Once inside her room, Crystal stood leaning against the wall, listening to the sounds overhead. Footsteps, a mutter of conversation, doors opening and closing.

One must take precautions.

She knew now that Murdoch would find nothing upstairs. Gregg had already proved he could cover his tracks.

Thad Hoskins. Thad and his "carpentry work." Of course: all that banging and pounding last week had been Thad converting the staircase to closets, sealing them off. And sealing his own doom.

Overhead, the footsteps subsided. They were leaving the apartment now, coming downstairs again. Crystal hurried into the hall as they emerged from the doorway at the far end. She started forward to meet them halfway.

Gregg nodded at her pleasantly as they approached. "We can go back now," he said. "That is, if Mr. Glass is satisfied."

Crystal tried to catch Murdoch's eye, but he was already addressing Gregg.

"One more thing, before we go. About these rooms you have here for rental . . ."

Thank God he hadn't forgotten! Crystal breathed a silent prayer. *Please, please remember what I told you about the other staircase, the one behind number 17!*

Gregg nodded. "Would you care to inspect them? They're all alike—uniform construction."

"Then one will do." Murdoch turned, glancing casually at the numbered doors. "How about this?"

He was staring at number 17.

Gregg hesitated.

"Anything wrong?" Murdoch murmured.

"No." Gregg stood indecisively for a moment. "I was just trying to recall if it happens to be rented. I shouldn't wish to intrude upon a guest's privacy."

"Suppose you knock." Murdoch said.

Gregg frowned. "Yes, of course."

He knocked. And waited. The moment of silence seemed to stretch forever for Crystal. Gregg knocked on the door again. There was no response.

Murdoch merely stared patiently, waiting. Gregg met his stare, then shrugged. He turned slowly and inserted his key in the lock.

The door of number 17 swung open to reveal an ordinary room, like all the others. Like Crystal's room, with bed and bath, carpet and curtains, a window through which sunlight shimmered from the sanity of the street beyond.

Murdoch glanced through the doorway for a moment. "Looks very cozy." His voice was flat.

"We try to make things comfortable for our visitors." Gregg closed the door. "Now, shall we go downstairs?"

Murdoch nodded. He was making little marks in his notebook—meaningless marks, of course. There was nothing for him to note here, nothing at all. Then he put the notebook away.

Was it a final gesture? Had he called it quits? Crystal steeled herself for the sound of his voice. But it wasn't until they'd walked around the corner and back into the pharmacy that he spoke.

"I'd like to see the cellar now," Murdoch said.

Crystal glanced at Gregg, waiting for his reaction. His face was immobile. "I've not had time to straighten things out down there," he said. "I'm afraid it's rather a mess."

Murdoch nodded. "That's all right. I'm used to messes."

Gregg produced his key as he led the way along the pharmacy aisle. "This way."

They entered the dispensary, moving past Hickey, who was filling a prescription. Placing a funnel in a medicine bottle, he poured in a portion of the contents from a larger container labeled ELIXIR OF HEROIN. Crystal vaguely recognized the name: one of those new nerve tonics, milder than laudanum, they said.

Gregg was unlocking the door at the far end of the dispensary. Funny, she'd never even noticed it was there, but when it opened she saw the steps, flickering into focus as Gregg turned up the gas jet in the wall of the stairwell.

"Low ceiling," said Gregg. "Mind you don't bump your head."

He started down, and Murdoch followed. Neither man paid any attention to Crystal. Perhaps if she just stayed within the shadow of the stairwell, her presence wouldn't be noted. It was worth chancing: she'd come this far, and she had to see the rest.

Another gas jet flared up from below. Crystal's glance followed Gregg and Murdoch as they moved across the cement floor. In the soft light she saw the asbestos-girdled outlines of the furnace, the wooden sides of the coal bin, the pile of kindling heaped alongside it, shipping crates and wooden boxes lining the wall, awaiting disposition, the metal mouths of washtubs next to the boiler, a stack of old newspapers and magazines—and nothing more.

But Murdoch was pointing. "That door over there. Where does it lead to?"

"Outside." Gregg moved to it, grasped the knob, pulled the paneled surface forward. "For deliveries."

"I see."

Crystal watched as Murdoch crossed the concrete, his eyes noting the tangle of heating conduits overhead, extending like tin tentacles from the squatting octopus of the furnace. A skein of water pipes snaked into ceiling and wall. Now he thumped the wall. Its rough, unfinished surface gave off a reassuring ring.

Gregg nodded at his companion. "Satisfied?"

Crystal didn't wait to hear the answer. She edged back up the steps, out of sight, out of hearing. The tension drained away, leaving only the numbness of realization. She'd seen everything now, and there was nothing to see.

When they came up the stairs again she was standing there, pretending to watch Hickey as he affixed a label to the medicine bottle for some nice old lady.

Gregg's voice cut through her reverie. "Crystal! I didn't realize you were waiting all this time. Come along, we're going back to the office." He turned to Murdoch. "You have something for me to sign, Mr. Glass?"

Murdoch nodded.

As they went down the hall, Crystal managed to capture Murdoch's attention for a moment, though only for a moment, just long enough for her lips to shape the silent syllables. *Thad Hoskins. Alice Porter.*

Murdoch's eyes flickered.

Then they were in the office, staring at the figure seated behind the desk, the waiting figure that turned and rose to reveal a smiling, familiar face framed by ash-blond hair.

"Why, if it isn't Alice Porter!" said Gregg. "What a pleasant surprise!"

21

Some fish spawn in a few days. Rabbits and guinea pigs litter in a matter of weeks. The human embryo needs nine months to evolve, and the gestation period of the elephant is sometimes close to two years. The larger and more complex a life form, the longer it takes to multiply. With one exception. A newspaper produces a new issue every twenty-four hours.

In the newsroom outside Charlie Hogan's office, conception was a daily routine. By midafternoon, scribbling reporters had impregnated a thousand pages with ink; through the dinner hour, the rewrite men toiled over their tasks and the layout department went to work. Then the linotypers and printers took over for accouchement. As the evening advanced, the presses started to bear down, sending convulsive shudders through the building above as they labored for the next morning's delivery.

Tonight was typical, and Charlie Hogan's cubicle shook spasmodically in accompaniment to the birth pangs below. Closing the door invited claustrophobia in an area scarcely sufficient to accommodate Hogan himself. But somehow Crystal and Jim had also managed to squeeze into the space.

"It's true, then, what Crystal tells me." Jim glowered at Hogan across the desk, his voice rising above the din. "You did hire her back again?"

The city editor nodded. "Yes, on a special assignment."

"Is that what you call it, deliberately allowing her to take such a risk?"

"Now, darling," Crystal said. "There's no reason to get excited."

"Then why didn't you tell me what was going on?"

"Because I knew you'd be upset. And there's no need for it." Crystal turned to her employer. "I didn't mean for us to burst in on you this way. He insisted on coming."

"I wanted to make sure she was telling the truth." Jim's face was grim. "I've heard so many stories."

"But it is the truth!" Crystal put her hand on Jim's arm. "You can see now I was never in any danger."

"I can see you made a fool of me all along." Jim shook his head. "And for what? Genevieve Bolton is alive. Alice Porter is alive."

"Look here, now," Charlie Hogan said. "I don't want to butt in on your affairs, but whatever Crissie did, she was trying to help you. She wanted you to get your job back."

"It was her own job she was thinking about." Jim scowled. "If she'd just left matters well enough alone in the first place, there wouldn't have been any trouble."

"Please." Crystal broke in quickly. "If you'll only listen—"

Jim yanked his arm free. "I've heard enough." He nodded curtly to Hogan. "My apologies for intruding. Good night to you, sir."

"Jim!"

Crystal's voice was cut off by the bang of the door.

She bit her lip, then glanced at Charlie Hogan. "I'm sorry."

Hogan stubbed his cigar butt in the ashtray. "So am I, but he'll cool off when he's had some time to think things over."

"I didn't mean to hurt his pride."

"Don't take it so hard. We all make mistakes, and you thought you were acting for his own good." Hogan grinned self-consciously. "Remember, you had me convinced too. That makes us both wrong."

"But we weren't wrong!"

"Crissie, for God's sake, let's not start that again."

"We haven't finished." Crystal leaned forward over the desk. "He wouldn't listen to me, but you've got to."

"I'm due in the pressroom." Hogan pulled out his watch, inspecting it face to face. "Almost midnight."

She nodded. "I know. And I must get back before Gregg suspects. It's only because he took Alice Porter to dinner that I was able to get away this long."

"It doesn't matter anymore what he suspects." Hogan rose. "Tomorrow you pack up and get out." He nodded. "You did your best, but it just didn't work out. Come back to work on regular assignments and we'll just forget the whole thing."

"Suppose I can prove I was right?" Crystal's voice rose above the clangor from below.

"How? You saw this Alice Porter with your own eyes. If

she's alive and well, then there's no reason to believe any harm came to the others."

"Unless she's Gregg's accomplice."

"What?"

"I've been doing some thinking." Crystal's eyes narrowed. "Suppose Alice Porter was Genevieve Bolton?"

"You're not making sense."

"Yes, I am. After Alice and Gregg went off to dinner, I spoke to Mr. Hickey. He tells me Alice Porter was already Gregg's secretary before the castle was built. And the two of them were planning to be married."

"But Gregg was engaged to Genevieve Bolton."

"So he says."

"And your fiancé saw a letter from her to prove it."

"Suppose the letter wasn't really written by her? Gregg has a dozen specimens of her signature on documents she witnessed for him at the office. What's to have prevented him from sending a signature and a draft of a letter to Alice Porter in Saint Louis, with instructions to copy both and mail the forgery back to him?"

"Genevieve Bolton wasn't in Saint Louis. She went to Kansas City, and the letter was postmarked from there."

Crystal shook her head. "What if Alice Porter went from Saint Louis to Kansas City on Gregg's instructions? And, acting on Gregg's orders, she posed as Genevieve Bolton during her stay. Suppose it was really Alice who spoke to Jim's boss on the telephone?"

"What if?" Hogan shook his head. "You have no proof."

"Genevieve Bolton's body would prove it."

"If Gregg was smart enough to concoct such a scheme, he wouldn't leave evidence. If he's guilty—and I say if, mind you—he's managed to flimflam everyone, including the police. I know Stan Murdoch. He's nobody's fool."

"It was my fault Murdoch was misled. I should have guessed Gregg would seal up those staircases."

"What about room seventeen? You saw it with your own eyes."

"I saw a room, yes. But it couldn't have been seventeen. I think Gregg anticipated a search and switched numbers on the doors. It's easy: they all look alike. If Murdoch went out there again—"

"Murdoch's not going out again on your say-so." Hogan put his hand on Crystal's shoulder. "And if there's a speck of truth in all this, you're not going back either."

"Gregg won't harm me. Not as long as he believes that story about poor dear Mama and the money she wants to invest."

"But when he stops believing?"

"By that time I'll find what I'm looking for."

"You've been looking! What more can you do, steal his keys? Everything will be twice as difficult now, with this Porter woman on the premises."

"Maybe Alice Porter is our key. If they're in this together, she can open the doors for us."

"She's not going to talk. Give me one good reason why she should."

"You give me the reason." Crystal spoke quickly. "Put somebody on it, see what you can find out about her. Then get the information to me and—"

"No." Hogan frowned. "You tried that with Thad Hoskins and it didn't work. Besides, I don't want you involved. It's too risky."

"But think of the story."

"I'm thinking of you."

"It's perfectly safe, I told you that."

"I get it." Hogan shrugged. "Still worried about getting

Jim's job back for him, aren't you?" He turned away, silent for a minute. "All right, let me talk to the Chief, see how much he's willing to shell out for an exclusive like this. Maybe Alice will talk if the price is right. But we've got to size up the situation first."

"That's where I come in," Crystal said. "I'll keep an eye on her meanwhile."

"That's where you get out!" Hogan's jaw tightened. "The Chief's away and I won't be able to get hold of him until Monday. But you're not waiting around until then."

"If I don't go back tonight he'll get suspicious," Crystal said. "You know that."

"All right, but I want you out of there tomorrow."

"I'll still need a reason for leaving."

"And a damned good one." Hogan nodded, then snapped his fingers. "What was that name you gave him when you spun the yarn about your mother's attorney?"

"Mr. Pilchrist. But there's no such person."

"There will be, tomorrow." Hogan grinned.

"You?"

"That's right. Mr. Pilchrist from San Francisco, in town for the Fair. But he's going back immediately, and he's come to take you with him. Because poor, dear Mama wants you at home right away to make arrangements for that power of attorney you told Gregg about."

"You think he'll believe you?"

"Don't worry, I'll convince him. He'll want to believe me anyway because he's itching to get that money into your hands where he can control it. There'll be no problem; everything will happen so fast he won't have time to think. Once you're gone, you can stay away for a couple of weeks before he starts suspecting anything. By that time we'll have the goods on him."

"You think of everything, don't you?" Crystal smiled. "I don't know how to thank–"

"Never mind that." Hogan's voice was brusque as he glanced at his watch again. "I've got to get down to the pressroom now. But remember, I'm coming by for you tomorrow."

"What time?"

"Not too early–it's going to be almost daylight before I finish here, and I've got to get some sleep." Hogan rubbed his chin. "Besides, we want to make this convincing. If Gregg ever looks up the schedules, he'll see there's no train leaving for the West Coast on Sundays until nine o'clock. So suppose I show up at six."

"Good! That leaves me time enough to pack in a hurry, and no time for arguments."

"Then we're all set. Just sit tight until I get there."

"I'll sit tight," said Crystal. And then she ran.

22

THE MIRROR watched them from the wall. It peered across the room like a great glassy eye, searching the shadows of the canopied bed, and Gregg was conscious of it even as he bent over Alice.

She moaned slightly at his touch. And that was the way he wanted it: the bedroom belonged to him, she belonged to him, everything belonged to him. He'd earned it, and he was going to enjoy it—all this and more. Because he had the power, the power to make them all serve him.

Sudden pain slivered his shoulder. Gregg winced, pulled back and ran his hand across the scarlet slash.

"What the devil'd you do that for?" he muttered. "Can't

you see I'm bleeding? You ought to cut your nails."

"It wasn't a fingernail." Alice lifted her left hand, and he saw the sparkle of the stone on her ring finger.

"With the ring?" Gregg shook his head disgustedly. "You're drunk. Why didn't you take it off?"

"I'm not drunk." Alice raised herself on one elbow. "No thanks to you, the way you kept filling my glass all through dinner."

"Why did you cut me with that diamond?"

"Because it's not a diamond." Alice pouted, her lips a coral curl. "Where'd you buy it, the same place you got the mirror?"

"That's nonsense!"

"Ask Sheeny Mike. I stopped by while I was in Saint Louis and asked him to appraise this. He said it was one of the finest pieces of bottle glass he'd ever seen."

Gregg's eyes widened. "Alice, please, I swear I didn't know! I bought the ring from Angelo Riccardi—you've heard of him: the best fence this side of the Mississippi; paid him a good price. I never dreamed he'd swindle me."

"That'll be the day, when anybody swindles you!" Alice swung her legs over the side of the bed, blond braids tossing as she shook her head.

"Let's not quarrel over trifles." Gregg turned and reached for the bottle resting in the wine cooler beside him. "Here, let's have a drink."

He filled their glasses on the bed stand and handed one to her. She hesitated, then drank slowly, the anger in her eyes unappeased.

Gregg nodded. "That's better. Now don't worry about the ring—I'll get you another next week. And this time I won't deal with a fence."

Alice frowned at him over the rim of her glass. "Where'll it come from then, the same place you find all your other jewelry?"

"What's that supposed to mean?"

"Mike told me you've been sending him a lot of stuff since I left. Rings, necklaces, bracelets, brooches. One man's gold watch and chain and a signet ring, but all the rest of it women's jewelry. How come?"

Gregg shrugged. "You know I can't risk fencing anything locally: too easy to trace the items here. It's safer for me to work with someone out of town like Mike."

"That's not what I'm talking about, and you know it." Alice started to put down her glass, but Gregg refilled it quickly as she spoke. "You've been up to your old tricks again, haven't you?"

"Suppose I have?" Gregg fingered his moustache. "You know I built this place to attract Fair visitors. Tomorrow night the Fair will end, and there'll be no more opportunities. I've had to make hay while the sun shines."

"And after dark?" Alice's voice had a sharp, scorn-honed edge.

"Alice, Alice!" Gregg sighed wearily. "How often must I remind you that it's only business, the same as it was with you?"

"Never mind about me!"

Gregg ignored the warning. "I didn't ask any questions when I pulled you out of Carrie Watson's shooting gallery. I leveled with you about the setup here, made you a partner. And if you're going to start getting jealous at this late date."

"I'm not just your partner! We're going to be married! Or did you forget that little detail when you met Genevieve Bolton?"

"Bolton was an accident—I told you that." Gregg spoke

patiently. "If I hadn't sent her on her way, we'd both be in trouble."

"You'd still be in trouble if it wasn't for me!" The blue eyes flashed. "All that business about forwarding a letter, chasing from Saint Louis to Kaycee on the night train just to be on hand for a phone call. Suppose someone caught on that I wasn't Genevieve Bolton? I could have landed in the clink."

"Believe me, I appreciate all you've done."

"And how do you show it? By turning around and hiring yourself another girl the minute I leave!"

"You've got it all wrong." Gregg refilled both glasses, then reached down and replaced the empty wine bottle with a full one that had rested in reserve on the shelf below. "I engaged this Wilson girl because I had to have some clerical help while you were still away."

"Clerical help? Oh, Gregg, what do you take me for?"

"It's the truth. I've never laid a hand on her. And now that you're back, I'll send her packing."

"You do that little thing." Alice gulped her drink. "You just do that."

Gregg shook his head. "Since when did you get so pious?"

"I'm not pious." Alice's blue eyes clouded with concern. "I'm scared."

"How many times have I told you there's nothing to be afraid of?" Gregg reached for her hand and squeezed it reassuringly.

"Too many." The hand pulled away warily. "You can't go on like this forever. Not with people starting to snoop around, coming here and asking questions. You owe everybody in town; maybe it'd be a good idea to pay off. It's worth a few spondulicks just to get rid of them. Now's the time to quit, while you're ahead."

"But I am quitting, the minute the Fair is over. We're selling the business, selling the building, clearing out of here for good."

"Where'll we go?"

"Anyplace you choose. We'll have enough cash to last us for a long, long trip." Gregg smiled. "A honeymoon."

"You really mean that?"

"Of course." Gregg reached for her hand again, and this time it didn't elude him. "What do you suppose I've been working for, taking all these risks?"

The clouded blue eyes seemed to have difficulty in focusing properly. A touch of presbyopia, Gregg noted, or was it merely the effect of the alcohol? But Alice's voice was still clear.

"Sometimes I wonder if you know yourself. It's almost as if you like doing it for its own sake. All this make-believe—"

"Have I ever tried to fool you?"

"Of course. Only it didn't work, did it?" Alice laughed, and while the words were clear, the slurring sound of her mirth betrayed her inebriation. "Good thing I can't be mesmerized, either. Or else by this time you might have—"

Gregg put his finger to her lips. The gesture was gentle, and so was his voice. "Don't even think such a thing. You know how I feel about you. You're different."

"Am I, Gregg? You really mean that?"

"Yes."

Her voice rose as his hand fell. "Maybe it's because I'm the only one who caught on to your tricks right from the first. But I still love you in spite of them."

"And I love you."

"You'd better not forget it." Alice nodded. "I'm the only one who knows the whole thing, and don't you ever forget that, either."

"Why should I? Between husband and wife there must be no secrets." Gregg leaned forward, grasping the neck of the wine bottle, satisfying himself that it was chill to his touch. "It's cold now," he said. "Do you want more?"

"Why not?" Alice gripped her glass. "This is a celebration."

Gregg groped in the slush of icy water surrounding the bottle until he found the corkscrew. He grasped its silver handle, then spiraled its convoluted steel shaft into the yielding cork.

Twisting, turning, tugging, Gregg uncorked the wine. Quickly he filled Alice's glass, then his own.

As she lifted her drink, Gregg stared at her over her shoulder in the mirror. Yes, she was different. Couldn't be fooled by the ring, couldn't be mesmerized by its glitter. No way to deceive her, no way to hypnotize, to control her demands and possessiveness. *I'm the only one who knows the whole thing, and don't you ever forget that, either.* A hard bargain and a hard woman.

The glass halted at her lips. "What are you looking at?"

"You." He smiled. "Blue eyes. Long golden hair. You remind me of another Alice. Alice in Wonderland."

She laughed. Brittle laughter, brittle and hard.

Drink me. That's what it said on the bottle, and Alice drank it and started to shrink. But that was in Wonderland. This Alice was hard, too hard.

He put down his own glass, staring at her directly, staring at the movement of her throat. His fingers curled around the silver handle of the corkscrew, gripped and thrust, dug and twisted into the soft neck.

Alice dropped her glass. Her eyes rolled back until only the whites showed and her head rolled back. Her neck was still white; he'd found the carotid artery, but the corkscrew plugged it, twisting deeper and deeper as she gurgled and then was still.

A few drops of blood oozed, but nothing reached the rug, nothing stained the sheets. He lifted her quickly but cautiously, before the sphincter muscles could relax and release. Mustn't happen here. No telltale discharge. This is Wonderland, not the stockyards. He moved to the mirror, holding Alice in his arms. His elbow found the catch embedded in the scrolled frame at the mirror's base, and he pressed against it.

The mirror swung silently aside, disclosing the dark aperture behind it. Tilting his burden forward, he dropped it down the narrow chute. *Goodbye, Alice. Goodbye to Wonderland. This is Through The Looking-Glass.*

He slid the mirror back into place. Glancing over his shoulder, he glimpsed the high cabinet in the corner, the locked cabinet. *Drink me. Eat me.* She hadn't learned the secrets of Wonderland after all.

Now, down the rabbit hole. Down the rabbit hole underneath the rug in the bathroom. No watch and no weskit—just a white rabbit scurrying through the burrows beneath, scurrying to its lair.

The lair where Alice waited, resting where she had fallen. Not completely white anymore, because of the tumble through the chute. But soon she would be clean again.

He did what was necessary then, and she was clean and soft once more. Soft and yielding, the way a woman should always be. And fair, so very fair.

But even clean she is a vessel of uncleanliness which must be discarded. Discarded, along with all these foolish fantasies. The party's over. No more Wonderland, no more Alice.

You're G. Gordon Gregg. You did what you've done before, did what you had to do, for a realistic reason. Did it to protect yourself. Self-preservation is the first law of Nature and you are a natural man. A professional man, a superior man, governed not by stupid, hidebound moral hypocrisy but by logic and intelligence. Always remember that.

Logically and intelligently, Gregg reached for the tools of his profession. And as he made the incision he remembered how it had been the first time, long ago, when he'd cut off the puppydog's legs.

23

LATE ON SUNDAY MORNING, Crystal awoke as church bells boomed. She had always hated Sundays, as a child. On Sundays everything changed. Daddy turned into a stranger, a man in black, preaching from the pulpit. And Crystal became a minister's daughter, sitting stiffly and silently in the front pew.

Sunday was dress-up day, be-quiet day, don't-play day, grown-up day. And after the sermon came the long and boring meal when relatives and guests talked among themselves; then the time of tedium when you squirmed and fidgeted with the visitors in the front parlor.

Crystal could still summon the scene in every detail: the

calling cards on a silver tray, the bowl of wax fruit resting on the table next to the stuffed bird under the bell glass. She remembered the aunts with their bustles and feather boas, the uncles in their stiff-collared Sunday best. How she used to stare at the grandfather's clock—the stern sentinel standing in the shadows, marking the moments and minutes and endless hours of monotony that were all Sunday ever offered.

But there was no grandfather's clock now, only the alarm here on the night stand. Crystal blinked at it in surprise. Almost noon; had she really slept that long? Of course, it had been late when she returned, and she'd been very tired. No sounds from upstairs had disturbed her slumber; if Gregg came home after she did, he hadn't made any commotion. She might still be sleeping now if it weren't for the bells.

As Crystal wriggled out from between the covers, their clangor ceased. Her slippers scuffed against the silence when she crossed to the window and raised the shade.

Sunday waited outside the windowpane. The old Sunday of childhood memory, the Sunday of gray gloom. Rain had fallen during the night, and the sidewalk below was still wet.

Dressing seemed to take forever, but once she finished, what would she do with her day? There was no Jim now to keep her company. Walking out on her like that last night—so unfair.

Unfair. Was that really all she felt? Where was the regret, the sense of loss? Crystal shook her head. Looking back, it was almost as though she'd known what would happen, expected Jim's reaction. What puzzled her was her own feelings; instead of sorrow there was something almost akin to relief. Jim hadn't understood; perhaps he never would.

In a way, he seemed a part of the past, part of the Sunday

world of her childhood. A world of *Speak when you're spoken to, Mind your manners, Children should be seen and not heard, A woman's place is in the home.* Nothing wrong with that world, but Crystal knew she didn't belong in it anymore. She'd broken out of the parlor and there was no going back.

But that didn't absolve her. No matter how Jim felt now, she still owed him something. She'd lost him his job, and that made her responsible for putting matters to rights again. And she intended to, with Charlie Hogan's help. By evening she'd be out of here for good and the plan would be under way. Now all she had to do was wait; that and nothing more. She'd given her word.

But there was nothing in the plan that said she had to go hungry today. No reason why she couldn't do what she'd done on other Sundays: go down to Bracton's on Sixty-third for lunch. Usually Gregg escorted her there, but since there was no sign of him now, she could still go alone.

Crystal busied herself with the bed—smoothing down the counterpane, tucking in the edges of the spread. That was Elsa Krause's job, really, but the new maid probably wouldn't be working on Sunday until afternoon. As she finished, she found herself wishing that Gregg *would* come knocking on her door. Anything was better than being alone on this dismal day. But he didn't knock, and there was no sound from above.

Shrugging, she went to the closet for her coat and umbrella. Too bad she couldn't pack now and be ready when Charlie Hogan arrived. But that would give away the show; better to wait. If only she could relax, stop feeling so edgy.

She glanced over at the clock. Almost one. If she took her time eating, it might be three when she got back. By then Gregg should be up and about, perhaps working on the books in his office. She'd make it a point to find him then, keep him company until Hogan showed up.

Once out on the street she was grateful for her coat, for the air was damp. But the skies seemed to be clearing. Crystal hurried along Sixty-third, mingling with the churchgoers returning from late services. Some of them were already seated over luncheon when she arrived at Bracton's, and it was surprising how familiar they seemed. As Crystal glanced around the restaurant's low-ceilinged dining room she could almost believe she was back home again for dinner. The surroundings were different, but the guests remained recognizable. Here were the aunts in their floral hats, the uncles in their too-tight toggery; and here, too, was the chatter and rumble of Sunday socializing.

A waiter led her to a table. She seated herself, scanned the menu, ordered, and still the illusion persisted. When Crystal finished eating, she could almost believe that in a few moments she'd be going into the parlor for another long, dull afternoon.

Until she looked up and saw Gregg moving toward her table.

"I hoped I'd find you here," he said.

Gregg wore black today, but it wasn't the black of mourning. The suit with the welted lapels was Sunday best, and so were the spats, the gloves, the bowler. With his waxed moustache he looked very much the boulevardier as he seated himself opposite her and waved a summons to the waiter.

Scanning the menu, he gave his order quickly, then glanced up across the table. "Sorry I missed you," he said. "I meant to stop by and invite you to lunch, but there wasn't a free moment. It seems everyone is checking out today, now that the Fair is ending."

"Hard to believe it's really over," Crystal murmured.

Gregg smiled at her. "You really didn't get much of an opportunity to see it, did you? I thought we might go for a last look this afternoon."

Crystal hesitated. But it was still quite early, and spending a few hours at the Fair would help make the time go quickly. Hogan wouldn't be coming until six; she'd make certain they were back by then.

"I'd like that," she said. "But if you're busy—"

"Everything's attended to. We can have the rest of the day to ourselves."

The waiter returned with a full tray, and Gregg prepared to eat. "With your permission," he said. "I'm famished."

He must have been, because he'd ordered chicken. Crystal watched as he busied himself with carving the portion on his plate. Strange, she'd never noticed it before: his table manners were impeccably correct, his conversation continued in a casual flow, his dignified deportment was that of a model gentleman at dinner—but his hands seemed to have a life of their own. In his deft grasp the knife became a scalpel, slicing swiftly into the white meat, separating breast from bone with a precision born of surgical skill. It was an act of dissection.

Or was she letting her imagination run away with her? He seemed so calm, so poised. His use of a fork was delicate; his movements, as he lifted a morsel to his lips, were decorously deliberate. Then the mouth beneath the moustache opened to accept the fragment of flesh, the white teeth tore, the muscles of the lean jaw rippled convulsively, voraciously. The hands belonged to a surgeon, the face was that of a gentleman, but the appetite was animal.

Crystal glanced away quickly. It was reassuring to see the prosaic surroundings now, the family gatherings fresh from worship and ready for recreation to come; the sound of a baby crying at a table nearby was not an irritation but a comfort. She welcomed the very dullness she decried; anything was better than the feeling of being alone with this man.

Gregg's napkin moved over mouth and moustache, then crumpled and descended to the side of his empty plate. But the plate wasn't entirely empty: gleaming under the light was a little pile of bones.

"Shall we go?"

Crystal nodded quickly, eager to be off. Since when was she getting morbid over a silly thing like a chicken dinner? Here was Gregg, paying the bill, tipping the waiter, pulling back her chair and assisting her to rise. A perfect gentleman, and only a gentleman. If there was an animal within, it had been appeased.

"The weather's cleared. I thought we might walk over."

"That's a good idea."

Apparently others shared the notion, because the sidewalks were packed with pedestrians moving east. Even so, families on foot moved more swiftly than passengers in hacks and carriages; vehicular progress was less a parade than a funeral procession. Which in a way was appropriate, because the Fair was dying.

And yet there was no hint of an impending end as they neared the grounds. The autumn air was chill, but the skies had cleared and the White City rose resplendently against the background of blue.

Bands blared as they entered through the Midway gate, moved into the crowded commotion of the Plaisance. Suddenly Crystal found herself before the Street in Cairo. She frowned up at the ornate facade; had it really been only a few months since she'd first entered that garish gateway?

Threading their way through the crowd, they started to

retrace their steps. "Too many people." Gregg's voice rose above the din. "Let's get out of this."

He led her past the Moorish Palace, into the line before the Ferris Wheel. Slowly they inched their way toward the ticket booth until Gregg finally purchased admission with a Columbian half-dollar.

And then at last they were free, soaring above the shining spires and sun-dappled domes of this miniature world. Crystal glanced at Gregg. "I've been meaning to ask you," she said. "Will there be any change in my duties from now on?"

"Why should there be?"

"I was just wondering. Miss Porter used to be your secretary, didn't she? And now that she's back—"

"But haven't I told you?" Gregg shook his head. "Alice has the offer of a position with some firm in the East. She only stopped by en route to say hello, for old times' sake."

Crystal gripped the guardrail as the wheel dipped with a sickening sway. "Where is she staying?"

"Nowhere. I put her on the train after dinner last night."

The wheel whirled, and Crystal felt her whole world was whirling.

Gregg was staring at her.

"Something wrong? You're not ill?"

"No." She shook her head swiftly. "Just the motion."

The dark eyes probed. "By the way, how did you happen to know that Alice had been my secretary?"

Crystal searched for a safe answer, but there wasn't any. The wheel had spun, the world had turned and suddenly nothing was safe any more.

"Mr. Hickey and I were talking. He mentioned it."

The world whirled, but the dark eyes were steadfast, fixed on her face. "What else did he tell you?"

No way to avoid the eyes, avoid the answer. "He said you and Miss Porter once had an—understanding."

"I see." Gregg nodded. "So that's what's been troubling you, is it? No wonder you haven't seemed quite yourself today."

"It's really none of my affair."

"On the contrary. It's very much your affair." Gregg's hand gripped her arm. "Since you know about the understanding, as you call it, you might as well know about the misunderstanding." Gregg's voice was soft. "Alice didn't really leave last night to take another job."

Crystal caught her breath, and he nodded.

"I must confess the truth. She left because I told her I couldn't marry her. I told her that I was in love with you."

24

Charlie Hogan rounded the corner of Sixty-third and moved hastily along Wallace Avenue. He was tired, he'd nicked himself shaving and his socks didn't match. But here he was, rushing down the street, squinting at his watch, swearing under his breath.

Only four o'clock, he told himself. *What's your hurry?*

Damn foolishness, jumping the gun this way. Didn't put the paper to bed until sunrise, didn't put himself to bed until breakfast time. That was the real reason he'd told Crissie he wouldn't be out to get her until six; a man needs his sleep.

Only he hadn't slept, not a wink. Lying there, tossing and turning, thinking about G. Gordon Gregg and his crazy castle, thinking about Crissie. If what she said was true . . . but it couldn't be, of course. Most likely the worst Gregg had been up to was some kind of insurance fraud. No evidence of foul play. On the other hand, if he was mixed up in a swindle and he suspected Crissie knew, there might be trouble.

Either way, high time for her to get out of there. He should have put his foot down last night when she insisted on going back. Could have thought of a dozen other ways to handle it, all kinds of excuses for her to give. But he had the Sunday edition on his mind and he'd let her go. Damned foolishness letting her go; damned foolishness worrying about it and losing sleep.

So like a damned fool, he got up and dressed. And came out here on the El, two hours early. The pharmacy was closed, everything shut tight. But the Wallace Avenue entrance would be open for the convenience of the paying guests.

Hogan headed for it, moving along the deserted sidewalk under the fading rays of the late-afternoon sun. Halting before the doorway, he reached into his pocket for the note pad on which he'd scribbled during his ride. Better make sure he remembered.

Pilchrist head of Frisco firm? Give fake address—Geary St. If Gregg suspicious of Crissie leaving immediately, say her mother is ill.

Hogan nodded to himself. Good thing he'd thought about that illness angle; it was a convincing touch if he needed one. Because Crissie was coming away with him no matter what.

Shoving the pad back into his pocket, he yanked open the door and marched up the stairs. The upper landing was dark as a tomb. Ought to turn up the gas.

Hogan peered down the empty hall; its doors stood dim and silent in a double row. Which room was Crissie's? Number three, she'd told him. Here it was. He knocked, and the sound echoed along the corridor.

No answer. Try again.

"Crissie?"

There was a response then, but it came from behind him. The door across the hall opened and a pudgy face peered up, framed by a shawl.

Hogan stared at the woman as she emerged from the doorway, clutching a shabby reticule.

"Was ist's?"

"I'm looking for Miss Wilson."

"Ja. Iss not here. They all go today." She nodded. "I go too, but I come back." She patted her reticule. "I forget it ven I finish der cleaning."

Hogan nodded. *The cleaning woman. What was her name, now?* "You're Mrs. Krause?"

"How you know?" The pudgy face furrowed in a pudgy frown.

"Crissie—Miss Wilson—told me."

"So." The frown faded. "You are a friend, *ja?"*

"That's right. And I've got to see her. It's very important. You got any idea where she might be?"

"She goes this noon. Maybe by the Fair."

"And Dr. Gregg?"

"He iss gone also." She nodded. "Later, he vent."

"Do you know when either of them will be back?"

Mrs. Krause shrugged. "Tonight." Turning, she closed the door and stepped out into the corridor. "You come again."

"Yes, I'll do that."

Hogan turned and moved down the hall. Mrs. Krause followed directly behind him. At the foot of the stairs he held the door open for her.

"Are you going to the Fair now?"

"Nein." Mrs. Krause shook her head firmly. "Too much valking. My feet they are already sore."

Together they moved along the walk toward Sixty-third Street. Mrs. Krause started for the curb at the crossing, then glanced back. "You come tonight maybe?"

"Yes, thanks."

Hogan waved and headed in the opposite direction. The pharmacy was closed, the castle was deserted. Paying guests gone, Gregg gone. And Mrs. Krause had closed the door across the hall from Crissie's room. *Closed, but not locked.*

The coast was clear. He glanced over his shoulder, just in time to see Mrs. Krause board the waiting cable car at the corner. A bell clanged and the car pulled away. Hogan waited until it was out of sight, then retraced his steps. Rounding the intersection again, he moved down Wallace Avenue to the entrance.

Once more he consulted his watch. Not yet four-thirty. Crissie would keep her word and be back by six, but where was Gregg? Perhaps he'd spend the evening at the Fair, since this was the last night. But even if he didn't, chances were that he'd dine out before returning to the castle. In any case, now was the time to look around—provided there was anything to see.

Hogan entered and ascended quickly. The upper hall was dark and still. He went directly to the door opposite Crissie's room, reached for the doorknob, felt it turn easily in his grasp. The door swung open, and he stepped inside.

Glancing around, he catalogued the contents of the room. One brass bed, neatly made up. Night stand with an enameled pitcher and washbasin; the thunder mug was on the shelf below. Chiffonier against the wall—drawers empty. Nothing here, nothing in the bathroom. On the far side of the bathroom, another door leading to the room beyond. It was locked.

Hogan shrugged. Why not? Naturally connecting bath doors would be locked. He crossed the hall to number seven. Again the knob rotated and the door yielded. The interior was similar to the one he'd just inspected. Only difference was a picture on the wall. Bad litho of Rosa Bonheur's *The Horse Fair.*

Hogan went down the corridor, opening and closing doors at random. Number nine had a picture too, an unoriginal Canaletto. Number twelve had no picture, and the chamber pot was under the bed. And number thirteen was *locked.*

He rattled the knob, but it held firm. Then he knocked. Maybe Mrs. Krause was wrong: a guest might have stayed on. Hogan knocked again. Still no response. He started to turn away, then hesitated. Nothing to lose, was there? After a self-conscious glance along the hallway, he stooped and peered through the keyhole.

The room beyond was dark. Funny, it was on the street side and all the rooms had windows. There'd be daylight here, unless somebody had pulled down the shade. But he didn't see a shade: too dark to see anything, at first. Until his eyes found a focus on the stairs.

There was no room. Just a flight of stairs behind the door, leading upward. What had Crissie said about switching the numbers on the doors? Was the story true after all?

Hogan rose, glancing down the shadowed hall. Trespassing was one thing, but breaking and entering was another. On the other hand, he still had time. And a story was a story. Damn it, he had to find out; that was what mattered.

He took a deep breath and put his shoulder to the door.

25

The café was crowded, every table occupied, and the waiters fought their way through the crush. On the raised dais a string trio pitted Ethelbert Nevin and Chaminade against the clamor, but to no avail.

Gregg raised his glance across the corner table. "You're not eating."

"I can't." Crystal shook her head. "It's still so hard for me to realize—"

"I know." He smiled quickly. "Believe me, my dear, I hadn't intended to tell you this way. But sometimes one has no choice." He reached for her hand. "If you feel cheated of a courtship and a proper proposal, at least I promise to make up for it in the future. What would you say to a honeymoon abroad?"

Crystal stared into the dark eyes, and Gregg nodded.

"I was thinking of Europe, but perhaps you might prefer the Orient. We could leave by way of San Francisco and visit your mother before we sail. Would you like that?"

She hesitated. "Must I decide now?"

"Of course not. We have plenty of time." His hand gripped hers firmly. "A whole lifetime for the two of us. If you only knew how I've waited for this moment . . ."

Crystal listened, hearing the inner echo of her own response. *But he's so obvious—is this really the way he got around those other women? What fools they must have been! And so is he. No need to be afraid of him.*

"—been meaning to give you this," Gregg was saying. With his free hand he extracted something from his vest pocket. Before Crystal could follow his swift movement, he'd found her finger, and she felt the cold circle slip over it and lodge tightly against the flesh.

Then his grasp relaxed and she stared down, down at the diamond dazzle of the ring.

"Do you like it?"

She nodded; there was no other possible response to such blazing beauty. And now he took her hand again, raising it to his lips, the moustache tickling her fingers.

Despite herself, Crystal was impressed: the stone was so huge. Had this been the way he'd wooed the others? Had they too received such gifts? If so, they hadn't enjoyed them for long.

The thought came chillingly: suppose this was the only one? A single ring, offered to each in turn, only to be removed and bestowed upon the next. For an instant she panicked; then recollection brought reassurance. She wasn't like the others: she had protection. Stopping here for an early bite had been her idea; she had to get Gregg back to the castle before six, in time to anticipate Charlie Hogan's arrival. She could breathe easier then, because she'd be safe.

She was safe enough for the moment, too—safe enough to smile when Gregg suggested they leave.

"Let's get over to the lagoon," he said. "If we're early, we can find a good spot to watch the fireworks. I understand there'll be a special display this evening."

It was already getting dark as they emerged, but the White City, bathed in incandescence, hurled an electric challenge to the sullen sky.

Gregg glanced up at the pall above the glowing glory. "We're due for some more rain tonight."

Crystal watched the passing crowd converging on the Mall entrance to the main fairgrounds beyond. "It doesn't seem to matter to people," she said. "After all, it's the last night."

"Their last night." Gregg smiled down at her. "But for us, it's the first." He took her arm. "Shall we?"

Crystal hesitated, framing the immemorial excuse. "Do we really have to stay?"

Gregg's smile vanished. "Something wrong?"

"Nothing, really. A slight headache." She nodded bravely. "Of course, if you really want to see the display—"

"Nonsense." Gregg moved forward. "You're quite right. I don't like the idea of fighting this crowd. And if it should start pouring, we'll be safely home."

Home. He means the castle. Crystal caught her breath, then reminded herself that Hogan would be waiting there. She was doubly thankful for that now, in view of what had happened. All the more reason for getting away while she could: if Gregg had plans for his fiancées, she didn't want to learn about them firsthand.

The thought sustained her as they forced a path to the exit. When they reached it, Crystal glanced back for a final glimpse of the grounds.

Looming against the light, the Fair seemed to encompass an endless expanse where half a million people milled amid the marvels of the past and the modern miracles of today.

The World's Fair. How could one believe it would ever end? And yet it must: the lights would flicker and die tonight; all the little lives gathered here would flicker and die in their own time. The modern miracles would merge with the past marvels. Soon it would be nothing but ancient history, as remote as the reality of Columbus himself. What had this land looked like four hundred years ago? Nothing but swampy meadow, lightless and lifeless. Perhaps it would look like that again four hundred years from now. *God, how quickly we all go down to dust.*

"Wuxtry! Wuxtry! Read alla bout it!"

The newsboy's cry jarred Crystal to awareness as they came out on the street.

"Extra, at this hour?" Gregg frowned, then called to the boy. "Here." He fished for a coin, took the paper in exchange, unfolded it. His eyes narrowed as he scanned the headline.

"What is it?" Crystal said.

"Carter Harrison is dead." Gregg read rapidly, shaking his head. "Assassinated, shot on his own doorstep by an unidentified man. They think it was someone who'd been turned down for a civil service job—"

Crystal listened as Gregg's voice rose. "It's an outrage!" He crumpled the paper angrily. "What's become of law and order? Shooting down a decent, respectable citizen like that —no one is safe anywhere. Why can't the police protect us from such maniacs?"

Gregg broke off abruptly. "I'm sorry," he murmured. "Come along; we'd better go before it starts to rain."

And then the decent, respectable maniac took her arm.

No one is safe anywhere. But suddenly, at the touch of his hand, she knew the one thing that would make her feel secure again. To walk down the street like this with Charlie Hogan.

As they started into the shadows, distant thunder rumbled in the west.

26

HOGAN MOVED up the stairs. By God, here it was, secret passageway and all! And at the top, Gregg's apartment, just as Crissie had described it.

The parlor light was on, and another light shone to the left. He decided to have a look in that direction for a starter and found himself in the private office. The first thing he noticed was the phony walk-in safe Crissie had told him about. Ignoring it, he located the strong-box behind the anatomy chart on the wall, but there was no way of figuring out the combination. And he couldn't force the locks on the files and desk drawers without leaving traces. Wasn't enough time to spare anyway; the main job now was to see as much as he could, get a general idea of Gregg's layout here.

Hogan went back into the parlor. Pretty fancy, with those rubber plants and the big organ. A tall cabinet, too, wide open, but nothing inside it except Gregg's liquor stock.

There was another cabinet in the dim-lit bedroom, a big brute of a highboy, but it was locked. Hogan turned away from it, staring at the gaudy bed and the big mirror. Looked like something out of a cathouse. Maybe that was where he'd got it. Hell of a job to install.

He moved up closer, running his hand along the frame, trying to see how it had been mounted. His knee hit the lower surface, and his foot kicked out instinctively before he could pull back.

Something clicked. And then the mirror was sliding away to the side, moving in its slotted frame to reveal the rough, unfinished lathwork of the wall behind it. And the dark, narrow opening below, a slanting chute downward.

Hogan squinted into the depths. Big enough to squeeze through, but you couldn't crawl along that hole; wasn't wide enough for movement, and there was nothing to hang on to. It was just a chute. Drop something in and let it fall, but where?

He stooped now, found the catch his foot had hit and released, activated it. The mirror slid back into place, and he stared into his own face: his shocked, startled face.

Must be a way of getting down below—stairs, probably, concealed like the chute behind the wall. Hogan started to thump the paneling, alert for a telltale hollow sound. He made a circuit of the room and found nothing. Nothing but the bathroom door.

What about a trapdoor, then? He threw back the rug; the bedroom floor was solid. Rearranging the floor covering carefully, he stepped into the bathroom beyond. Another rug here, but it was really just a bath mat. Almost casually, he kicked it aside.

And then he wasn't casual anymore. He found the trapdoor and the steps descending into darkness. Not utter darkness—there was a faint light somewhere below.

He started down slowly, making sure he had a firm footing on the narrow treads. So many stairs and then, when he came to the corridors below, so many tunnelways slanting down in the dim, yellowish haze of the gaslight, so many doors lining the passageway.

Hogan veered cautiously to his right, checking his landmarks as he went. Easy to get lost in this maze if you weren't careful. All these doors: they could lead anywhere, to every part of the castle. One, at what he guessed was ground-floor level, was locked; probably it connected to Gregg's pharmacy office. He made a mental note to investigate when he retraced his steps.

Rounding a corner, he halted suddenly, startled by a slit of light issuing from a crack in the wall. It was not until he moved closer that he realized he stood before another door, slightly ajar; if it hadn't been, he'd never have noticed, because the surface was identical with that of the wall on either side. Closed tightly, it could easily be overlooked in the shadowy tunnel.

Hogan came up to it, senses alert to sound or the hint of movement. But the musty corridor was silent except for his soft tread against the stone surface, and beyond the doorway nothing stirred.

He opened it, peering into the low-ceilinged room beyond. Just a cubicle lit by a wall jet flickering over the bare floor, the single wooden chair, the tiny table, the wooden shelving, the cot in the corner with its single blanket tangled and wadded to one side. Rough, paint-spattered work shoes rested beneath it, next to a discarded buttonhook and an empty pint whiskey bottle. A full complement of carpenter's tools was piled carelessly along the shelves.

Wasn't Thad Hoskins a carpenter? But he'd gone away. Left suddenly. Hogan frowned. Careless of Gregg, leaving these telltale traces behind.

Hogan backed into the passageway, closing the door, then followed the slanting slope down into deeper darkness. It was in the lower corridor that he found himself moving in the direction of the door ahead: the solid-oak door set flush in the wall at the far end of the tunnel.

Thunder sounded, faint and faraway. Hogan waited until the distant echo died, then halted before the door, straining to hear other sounds.

But there was only silence. Silence and shadow. And the door handle turning slowly and noiselessly beneath his fingers. The door, swinging open and inward to reveal the light from the cellar beyond. It had to be a cellar; this was basement level, or below.

Thunder boomed above, but Hogan didn't hear it.

He moved into the cellar.

27

LIGHTNING SPLIT the sky beyond the upstairs window.

"Don't be afraid," Gregg murmured, drawing the parlor curtains. "The storm is dying."

Crystal nodded. Now that the draperies were drawn, the parlor was frescoed with moving patterns of shadow and dancing light from the fireplace, glinting against glasswear, sparkling over beaded portieres, gleaming along the surface of the hassock on which she sat. Everything so snug and cozy here, but she was still afraid.

"You're sure you don't want a glass of wine?"

She glanced at the man in black, shaking her head, forcing a smile. Mustn't let him know how she felt. And mustn't feel that way. Gregg wasn't really a threat; not now, not for the moment. She had to remember that. As long as they were together like this he'd play his part, waiting for her to get that power of attorney. He'd play his part and all she had to do was play hers. The loving fiancée.

But it was past six, way past six now, and where was Charlie Hogan? He'd promised to be here—had something gone wrong? There must be a reason for his delay; she couldn't believe that he'd forget.

"I still can't believe it," Gregg said.

Crystal blinked. "Believe what?"

"That you're really mine." He smiled and sipped his wine.

"I know how you feel," she said. And meant it. She couldn't believe her own ears. Had he really deluded all those women with this rubbish, this dialogue straight out of a Bertha M. Clay romance? The waxed moustache and ever-so-refined mannerisms—these were the attributes of the "genteel" hero of a nickel-library scribble for servant girls.

But the other women weren't servant girls. What had they seen in him? What attraction had they found in the brilliantined hair, the set smile in the waxen, too-white face? In his black coat he looked like a miniature figure of a bridegroom atop a wedding cake.

Perhaps that was the answer. Young or old, spinsters or widows, most women wanted a husband. A handsome husband who could offer security. And once he realized this, Gregg had only to play his role—the role he knew so well; the role he was playing now.

"I've been thinking, my dear," he said. "We'd better make some plans. Not just for our trip, but for when we return. You'll be needing a maid, of course, and someone to tend to the cooking as well."

"Won't that be terribly expensive?"

"Let me worry about the expense. I'm not exactly a pauper, you know."

Crystal nodded. It was easy to respond to his make-believe, play her own part as he expected. If only she knew what was delaying Charlie . . .

"And another thing," Gregg was saying. "There's no carriage house here, but I know of an excellent livery stable down the street. We could have a rig of our own and keep the horses there." He broke off abruptly. "You're not listening."

"But I am," said Crystal, quickly. And she was: listening for a distant bell, a knock, the sound of Charlie's arrival.

"Poor darling." Gregg's smile was understanding. "You still have that headache, don't you?"

Crystal nodded, grateful for his misinterpretation. "I'm afraid so."

Gregg put down his glass and started toward her. "Let me help you," he said.

At the touch of his hands on her shoulders Crystal rose, turning to face him. "Try to relax," he murmured. The hands rose, converging at her temples. "Now, close your eyes."

She obeyed, because it was easier that way; easier to conceal her tremor at his touch. But then the hands began to stroke her forehead and the tremor ceased. The sensation *was* soothing; she did feel relaxed.

"That's better." His voice was soft, sympathetic. His hands were soft and sympathetic too, gently cradling her neck, easing the tension with their warmth. It was easy to close her eyes this way and accept his nearness, easy to respond . . .

Too easy. And it was only with effort that she whispered, "You can stop now. The headache's gone."

The hands halted. "Good." The hands halted, but did not drop away.

Crystal opened her eyes now, wondering why he hadn't released her.

"So much for my professional duties." Gregg smiled. "But there are other duties, too," he murmured. "The personal and private ones. The duties of a husband to his wife."

And now his hands were moving across her back, descending to her waist. It was as though he had reacted to her touch as she had to his, so that the mood of make-believe was melting, merging into something else. Hard to remember this was only pretense because his hands, so deft, so skilled, knew just where to press and caress, and his eyes . . .

She'd forgotten about his eyes, the deep, dark eyes. Not the painted stare of a doll on a wedding cake, but a living presence that held and hungered like the hands. And it wasn't playacting anymore, not when he touched her and she felt the sudden, terrible vitality flowing from his fingertips; not when his mouth crushed hers so that their mingled breath became a single panting of purpose and his heartbeat hammered against her own in a mounting, relentless rhythm.

No—I don't want this, said the voice from deep inside. But the voice was faint and faraway, the harsh breath drowning it out, and the heart was pounding and pulsing here and now. Here, as he lifted her in his arms, and now, as he carried her into the bedroom toward the canopied bed.

Taken by surprise. But was it surprise? Hadn't she known all along, even from the first time she saw him, that this was what she wanted? Wasn't that the reason she hadn't been able to banish him from her thoughts, the real reason she'd kept coming back? Not to save those other women but to be one of them?

She felt his caressing fingers suddenly stop.

What's that?

The dim bedside lamp flickered, faded, flared again.

"Wait," he whispered.

And then he rose, turned, hurried across the room. She lay listening as his footsteps receded through the parlor beyond, the hallway past it. There was a distant creak of a door opening and closing, then silence.

She was alone once more, yet not quite alone. For now, as she stared up at the shadows, fear came to join her.

28

Hogan moved into the cellar, then halted. He stared at the tile floor with the gutter bordering the walls. Runoff channels radiated to it from beneath a marble-topped slab set in the center of the chamber under an electric light.

Then Hogan saw what was on the slab: saw what stained it, dried and crusted, darkening the tiles and gutter alike. Saw the rust red, smelled the reek.

It rose all around him, the acrid odor, the stench of decay. And the light gleamed on the surgical knives scattered across the marble tabletop, winked wickedly over the scalpel and trocar and razor-toothed bone saw.

Cellar? This was a butcher shop.

He came into it cautiously, peering at the shelving set in

the wall beyond the table. More instruments littered its length, and behind them rose a row of jars and vials. Lined along the floor beneath were glass bottles and metal canisters.

Hogan stooped and examined the scrawled lettering of the labels taped to the sides of the containers. This was no drugstore stock of asafetida, calomel or smelling salts; all he saw here was solutions that preserved or destroyed.

Moving across the oblong chamber, he almost stumbled over the coil of rubber tubing that snaked along the floor from the outlet in the far wall. A hose connection—that was what it was; yes, here were the valve and nozzle. The water pipes would be overhead.

Hogan glanced up past the burning bulb. Something about the electric light disturbed him, but only momentarily. There was no time to think about it, not when he saw what yawned beyond.

The square dark opening set in the stone ceiling was centered directly above the marble slab. Anything dropped through it from overhead would land directly on the tabletop.

So there were at least two ways to reach this room: either along the route by which he came or through the opening. Whatever was meant to rest on that marble surface could be dragged if necessary, or else dropped from an upper floor. No need to wonder what happened after the tabletop was occupied; even a dull imagination could guess why the knives were sharp.

Butcher shop. Stockyard. Cut and saw, then use the hose to wash away the stains. But what happened then? Hogan scanned the solid tilework of the floor. No openings here, nothing concealed under the glare of the light. But on the wall opposite the shelving, the fourth wall . . .

On the fourth wall was a square of steel, set at waist level;

perhaps two feet in diameter, like the door of a furnace.

That was it, of course. Beyond the fourth wall was the rest of the cellar. The ordinary cellar, with its pipes and coal bin and furnace. And since the wall was solid, no one entering the regular cellar would suspect that this room existed behind it. No one would suspect that the furnace had two doors—the visible opening in the other cellar through which coal was shoveled, and the hidden door on this side. What fed the furnace from here?

He crossed to the wall and reached for the door handle set in the surface of steel. As he did so the thunder echoed again, distantly disturbing, like his unfinished thought about the electric light.

Then the door was open and he stared in at the fire. A fire, in this heat? Yes—the furnace had been banked low, but there had been a fire within the last twenty-four hours, and a bit of it was still smoldering. Smoldering and alive.

Tiny tongues of flame licked out delicately at charred black and gray coals. And there were other things to feed on that were not black, not gray, but white. Small splinters, larger shafts and one big rounded object resting on top, peering out at him with hollow eye sockets, grinning through flickering flames.

Hogan saw it clearly in the light from behind and above—the light that had disturbed him because it shouldn't have been here at all, not in an empty room.

Then he straightened to turn, sensing the presence behind him—turned to see who had entered with footsteps muffled by the thunder.

As he looked up, the thunder rose.

And so did the arm wielding the length of pipe.

29

GREGG LET THE PIPE fall. As it clattered against the tiles, he stooped over the body sprawled before him and ran practiced fingers along the contusion. No blood, but considerable edema. Hard to judge the force of such a blow. In any case, the intruder was unconscious and would stay that way for some time.

But who was he? Gregg turned the man over, but found no answer in his face. A stranger—someone he'd never seen before. Cigar case in vest pocket here. Watch and chain. Engraving on back of watch: *Charles M. Hogan*. Never heard of him.

Wallet from inside jacket pocket. Brown leather, scuffed edges. Fourteen dollars in bill compartment. One card in card case. Press pass, made out to Charles M. Hogan, City Editor of—

Gregg scowled. A newspaperman?

First those idiots from the insurance company, then that damned special investigator sniffing around. And now a reporter. Something going on here, something very peculiar. Knowing his identity didn't help; if anything, it only raised new questions.

Gregg's scowl deepened. The answer to that was obvious enough: he'd been spying on the premises. And there could be no doubt about what he'd seen.

Because it was all here. The chute that dropped the bodies to the table, the acids for destroying telltale clothing labels, smudging features against possible identification, the surgical instruments for dissecting the remains, the furnace into which the dismembered fragments were fed to the flames.

Even a child could put two and two together, realize what had become of those who disappeared here in the castle. The fatuous female guests, greedy O'Leary, drunken Thad who couldn't be trusted to keep secrets, Genevieve Bolton who trusted him too much and Alice Porter who didn't trust him enough.

Yes, a child could guess, but a child would never get this far. And it was no child who'd come here tonight. Thank God he'd had the sense to install that wiring circuit at the cellar doorway; opening the door caused the light to dim in his office and in the apartment upstairs. If it hadn't been for the signal, he never would have known about this intruder. This meddling bastard of a reporter.

But the questions remained. Why had he come? How had he found his way to this room? Only one possible answer. He was sent here. Told to come, by somebody who knew.

But those who knew were dead; all of them were dead. Nobody knew now, except himself. Unless there was someone who guessed, someone who suspected.

Gregg felt the perspiration breaking out on his forehead. Cold sweat. He frowned, gnawing his moustache. Mustn't panic now. Stop and think. There's got to be a solution. . . .

Automatically his hand dipped into the intruder's outer coat pockets, emerged with discoveries. A box of matches. Loose change. Cigar clipper, handkerchief, key ring. A pencil stub and a note pad. He riffled through the pages until he came to the scrawled sentences, sentences that didn't make sense.

Pilchrist head of Frisco firm? Give fake address—Geary St. If Gregg suspicious of Crissie leaving immediately, say her mother is ill.

Crissie? He read the final sentence again, until it registered. And then everything was crystal-clear.

30

A MOMENT after Gregg closed the distant door, Crystal rose from the bed. Her legs trembled; her throat was dry. She stood swaying before the big mirror on the wall, then closed her eyes to avoid the sight of her own image.

My God, what am I doing here?

No need to ask the question. No need to tell herself what might have happened, what would have happened, if Gregg hadn't left when he did.

But he had left. She could open her eyes now, because she was alone. Alone and herself again. No time for recriminations. It hadn't happened, and it would never happen, not now.

She wondered where he had disappeared to. Could

Charlie Hogan have arrived? She remembered the way the bedside lamp had flickered; perhaps it was some kind of signal to signify the presence of someone entering the corridor on the floor below where the guest rooms were located. If Charlie came, that was exactly where he would go to look for her. In which case Gregg would be bringing him up here. Of course, there'd be the explanation first—the business about Mr. Pilchrist from San Francisco.

Would Gregg believe it? He'd have to; but even if he had doubts, there was no danger. Once he realized that his visitor knew Crystal was here, he had no choice except to bring him to her. Charlie wouldn't be put off by any cock-and-bull story Gregg might concoct.

Crystal turned away from the mirror, noting the closet on the side wall, door ajar. Sudden impulse carried her across the room, impelled her hand to the door handle. The closet swung open.

That was what it was, and nothing more. No skeletons in Gregg's closet. Just a long row of garments, carefully hung, perfectly pressed. Odor of mothballs. Odor of sanctity. Clothes make the man, the proper gentleman.

Crystal let the door swing back, then moved, mouse-quiet, to the bureau across the arched doorway from the hall. The big brass-handled doors opened silently, revealing sartorial secrets. Crystal inspected an array of detachable collars and matching cuffs. She combed through cravats, lifted linens. Here were stacks of silk shirts, handkerchiefs monogrammed with the initials *G.G.G.*, piles of undergarments. In the bottom drawer, amid a clutter of socks, garters, spatterdashes and odd braces, she glimpsed a gleam of silver, clutched a coil of coldness.

And drew out, by its snub barrel, a pearl-handled revolver. A gentlemanly weapon, this: small, delicately made—

and fully loaded. For a moment she held it gingerly, uncertainly, as though weighing it and her decision. Then Crystal shifted her grip to the butt of the weapon, finding reassurance in its chill feel beneath her fingers.

Closing the drawer quietly, she glanced past the mirror to the far corner where the huge mahogany highboy stood in shadow, its double doors meeting beneath a metal mount from which a lock dangled. Its steel surface reflected a curlicue of dim light—a curlicue that was almost the shape of a question-mark.

On the near side of the cabinet, beneath the draped window, was a small night stand with a candle resting atop it in a pewter holder. There was a door in the base of the stand, but no lock depended from it.

Clutching the revolver, Crystal stopped before the stand and opened the door with her free hand. As she had expected, the interior was shelved, but the shelves were utterly empty.

Conceivably there might be some sort of compartment concealed at the back or along the sides, but the light was too dim to aid detection. Perhaps if she lit the candle . . . A box of matches lay beside the pewter candle holder. Crystal made use of its contents quickly, grateful for the added light that flared through the shadowy room. She placed the little pearl-handled revolver on the night stand, lifted the candle holder, then glanced at what had been hidden beneath it.

Glittering in the reflection of the candle flame was a tiny silver key. Candle in her left hand, key in her right, Crystal moved to the cabinet looming from the corner. Carefully she probed the lips of the lock with the key tip, felt the metal mouth swallow the sliver of silver. A twist, and the lock sprang open.

The dark doors swung back. Lifting the candle, Crystal peered into the cabinet. Its shelves were deep, and from them rose the domes of bell jars, the shining cylinders of gleaming glass, each filled with a transparent fluid in which floated a rounded redness. Row after row of bobbing blobs, twisting and turning in the flickering light. No need now to ask what had become of Genevieve Bolton, Alice Porter and all the others.

Then the door behind her opened and Crystal turned to stare at the man who had won their hearts.

31

GREGG CAME into the room swiftly, then halted as Crystal lifted the revolver from the night stand.

For an instant he stared in shocked silence as the moving muzzle rose to level at his breast.

"Crystal—no—"

"Don't move!"

He halted and she took aim carefully, her finger tightening on the trigger.

"For God's sake . . ." His face was ashen. "You can't—not like this . . ."

Crystal hesitated, but the weapon didn't waver. She held it steadily as she lowered the candle holder to the top of the night stand with her left hand.

Gregg's mouth twitched. "Listen to me; you've got to listen!"

Crystal shook her head. "The way you listened to the others?"

He swallowed quickly. "There was no choice. They would have run to the police."

"Because you swindled them?" Crystal's voice was scornful. "Because you lied and cheated?"

"You don't understand! It wasn't swindling, it was a business matter. Building a place like this, carrying out my plans. You've got to find working capital, that's the primary rule of economics." Gregg gestured. "Look at the Fair and you'll see. The big exhibits—the steel industry, the railroads, textiles, armaments: don't you think the men behind them had to do their share of what you call swindling? Banking, insurance, real estate, I don't care what it is, you've got to look sharp, cut corners, take whatever steps are necessary."

"Including murder?"

"Where do you draw the line? When a factory shuts down and workers starve in the streets, what do you call that? What's your term for the mortality rate of children working twelve hours a day in the sweatshops? Do you know that the average coal miner drops dead before he reaches the age of forty?"

Gregg's voice rose, energized by emotion, and Crystal frowned. *He believes it, he really believes it! A businessman, dealing in death. A salesman, dedicated to making a killing.*

And for a single frightening moment it seemed almost logical, in the way a nightmare seems logical before the awakening. But then she glanced at the open cabinet and the awakening came quickly.

"No," she whispered. "That's not your reason."

He followed her gaze, staring into the dark recesses of the shelves where the contents of the jars circled slowly in veined and striated array.

"This is why you do it, isn't it?"

She read the answer in his eyes—the deep, dark eyes. The eyes that guided the scalpel, gloated over the workings of the knife, treasured the trophies hidden here. The eyes that stared at her now, taking her measure, searching out her own secrets. Strangely calm eyes, and a strangely calm voice.

"You're not going to kill me, are you?"

Her fingers tensed against the trigger, then relaxed. "I'm calling the police."

"Of course."

But there was no hint of apprehension in his voice, only a curious confidence. That was what was in his eyes now: a compelling conviction. Compelling and overpowering, like the darkness rising around her. The dark room, the dark cabinet, the dark eyes.

Abruptly she glanced away, seeking the bright reassurance of the candle flame. It wavered from the tip of the taper atop the night stand, radiating warmth and comfort.

"Perhaps it's for the best." Gregg's voice did not waver, but it was warm and comforting too. "This has been an ordeal, I know. You must be tired, very tired."

The voice was understanding, too. She was tired, bone-weary. The very effort of forcing herself to face him, holding him off, had drained her. She had to fight the strength she sensed in him, the strength she'd always known he possessed. The power, attracting her in spite of all she knew, the power within his eyes . . .

"That's right." So calm, so understanding. "Don't look at

me. Look at the candle. Don't you remember when you were a little girl, how they tucked you into bed and left the candle burning?"

How did he know that? But it was true . . .

"There, now. Tired, so tired. But not afraid any more. You can still see the candle, even though you can't move. Just watch the candle and everything will be all right. All safe and snug until you fall asleep."

The voice was getting blurred. And the candlelight was blurry too. Because she was falling asleep. Only she mustn't, no matter how tired she felt, no matter how heavy her arms were . . .

"Heavy," whispered the voice. "So heavy. You can't hold it anymore. But you don't have to hold it, do you? Because the candle is burning and you're safe now, so you can let it drop. That's right. Open your hand, let it go. Now."

Something fell from beneath her fingers. She scarcely felt it, and that didn't matter either. Because she was asleep and the voice was fading away, the flame was fading away, she was fading away. And her eyes were closing and there was a warm band around her neck that seemed to grow tighter and tighter.

Crystal's eyes opened and she stared—stared at Gregg's fingers encircling her throat. She clawed at them, feeling the pressure and the pain, the squeezing strength. Gasping, she raised her hands to claw at his face, and he tightened his grip, bending her back. She stumbled against the night stand, heard it fall, but Gregg's fingers bit into her neck, tighter, tighter, bringing blackness. Everything black now but his eyes.

Suddenly the fingers splayed, releasing their hold. Crystal gulped air, staring at his red reflection. She turned at the sound of the crackling rising with a swirl of smoke from the canopy bed behind her.

The candle lay where it had fallen when the night stand toppled, at the base of the bed. But more than its tip was flaming now; the bed itself was blazing, billowing. Fire raced up the hanging canopy, radiated across the carpet to the wall and the cabinet in the corner.

Gregg stooped to scoop up the revolver from the floor. Through the curling smoke she saw the muzzle rise and swivel toward her. The sound of the shot reverberated through the room, but before its echo died she was stumbling across the threshold of the bath, slamming the door. Her fingers fumbled, then found the lock, and for a moment she stood panting in darkness.

Then he was hammering from the other side, the butt of his revolver smashing at the panels. The door shook; in a moment he'd break through, and she was trapped. Trapped here in the dark, in the tiny room from which he'd entered when he returned.

But how could that be? He'd left through the hall, yet come back this way . . .

There was a crack as the door panel splintered. Through the narrow opening she saw Gregg's contorted face framed against the flames of the burning room behind him.

The reddish radiance flickered against the walls and across the floor as she turned and saw the dark opening that gaped at her feet where the rug was rolled away.

So this was how he'd come . . .

Gregg smashed against the splintered door and another panel dropped, widening the opening so that his arm came through. The arm, and the hand holding the revolver.

As he fired, she dropped to the floor, then clambered into

the hole. Her feet found the steps and she edged down, down into deeper darkness. From above she heard a crash as the door gave way.

Hastily she lowered herself, glancing ahead to see the faint light flaring and fanning from beneath. No need to glance up—her ears gave evidence enough. Gregg's footsteps on the flooring overhead, then the thump on the stairs. He was coming after her.

Crystal reached the corridor and turned, her body movement causing the gas jets to flicker along the winding walls. Which way now?

She started to run to the right, the sound of her own panting magnified and distorted here in the confines of the corridor. A sharp turn—and then a sharp crack from behind her. A shot shrieked and echoed through the tunnel. Then another—and another.

She ran down the sloping incline, hearing the thud of his pounding pursuit. And turned into another passageway, still leading down, somewhere between the walls. Narrower, with a lower ceiling, and only two tiny gas jets, one on either side of the slanting tunnel. Just enough light so that when she looked forward she could see the end of the passage ahead—the dead end of the blank wall.

Crystal whirled around, just in time to see Gregg appear behind her. Just in time to flatten herself against the wall as he fired again. The noise was deafening, and so was the *splat* of impact as the shot struck the far end of the tunnel beyond.

Gregg didn't move. He stood there at the mouth of opening, stood quite calmly, eyeing her through the shrouding smoke. Then, as the smoke cleared, he raised his weapon again.

She cowered against the side of the corridor, but it was no

use; even in the dim light he could see her clearly. He squinted down the barrel of the revolver, taking careful aim. His finger squeezed.

Crystal braced herself for the sound of the shot, eyes closed. And heard the click.

Gregg cursed as he hurled the empty weapon aside. She opened her eyes as it fell, saw him standing in the distance, a shadow looming against the gaslit walls. The hands of the shadow curled.

Now she could only huddle there and wait while he came toward her down the corridor, came with the hands that curled and clutched and choked . . .

She turned to run then, but there was nothing ahead but the blank wall. The slanting floor was solid; no trapdoor here.

Abruptly she saw it, lying at the baseboard to her left, just beneath the gas jet. Something discarded or forgotten by a workman, something rusty and corroded: a crowbar. Its prying edge was dull, but no matter; it was heavy, solid iron, and it would serve.

Crystal grasped it, then turned. She opened her mouth, ready to warn Gregg to keep back, but the words never came. Because Gregg was already retreating. He edged his way along the tunnel until he stood at its mouth once again.

Stood and smiled, and disappeared around the corner. Slowly she started forward. He'd be waiting there, she knew, waiting to spring out at her when she came abreast of the turning. But the bar was heavy in her hands, its solidity reassuring. And before he could wrench it away she'd move; just one blow was all she needed . . .

Something crashed before her, slamming down from the low ceiling ahead, and the opening before her disappeared.

A barrier had dropped down; a barrier of solid steel, set

flush with the stone walls. The corridor's mouth was closed. No way out ahead and none behind. She wasn't in a corridor any more. Now that the metal had dropped, the passageway was transformed into a narrow room. A dungeon cell deep within the castle's walls; a dungeon without doors or windows.

A dungeon of utter darkness. Because now the lights were going out. Crystal glanced up as the gas jets faded. Their glow died, blurred into black.

Was this one of the ways he disposed of his victims? Had he built the tunnel deliberately with a dead end, a section into which he could wall up a prisoner? How many had died here in the darkness, unseen and unheard, died in slow agony . . .

Not slow.

For then she heard the hissing and she understood. The hissing from the wall jets. No light now, only the gas pouring in. The gas with its sickly-sweet stench, its suffocating scent, perfume of death, filling the narrow chamber, filling the laboring lungs . . .

Crystal stumbled along the corridor to the far end, the dead end, gasping for air. The unseen fumes rose around her, their hiss mingling with the sound of her labored breath. The crowbar was heavy in her hands; angrily she hurled it against the blank wall at the end of the tunnel. It struck with a hollow thump, then clattered to the floor.

She stood utterly still. It had sounded as if the wall were hollow.

Crystal dropped to her knees, hands groping frantically for the length of metal. The gas burned in her throat and windpipe, but it wasn't quite so concentrated here; she still had strength.

Her fingers found the bar, and then she rose, rose into the

reek, and struck out at the wall. Struck as she gasped, struck as she coughed and choked, struck again as her senses swirled—then felt something give way as air flooded against her face. She filled her lungs, smashed out again.

The crowbar found a purchase and she pried upward, lifting the thin stonework and forcing it aside. Light fanned through the opening; the light of a corridor beyond. Reeling, she clambered through the narrow opening and into the other passage, leaving the fume-filled darkness as she stood panting for air until strength returned.

Her head throbbed and her vision wavered, but she could see the far end of this new tunnel—and the door opening on an area beyond.

Letting the crowbar fall, she started forward. Up the corridor. Past the doorway. And into Gregg's waiting arms.

32

As Gregg carried her into the cellar chamber, Crystal screamed and struck out at him. But his grip was steel. Panting, he pressed her down upon the cold, unyielding marble table, pressed and pinned her there, capturing her wrists behind her.

She gasped, fighting to free herself, but he twisted her arms, yanking them upward so that she could only writhe helplessly beneath him. Writhe and gasp and stare up at the electric bulb swaying overhead, in the shimmer of smoke surrounding it. Now she saw its source; the dark opening in the ceiling from which the acrid cloud curled forth.

Gregg saw it too, and his movements quickened, his free hand groping in frantic haste to the tabletop beside her.

Crystal stared at the scrabbling fingers as they closed around the shining handle of a surgical knife.

Once again she kicked out frantically, but he moved deftly to one side, then gripped her wrists more tightly as he forced her down. Head twisting, she could only scream as he brought the scalpel up, raising its razor edge, poising it to plunge.

Then suddenly the knife fell from his grasp, to teeter on the edge of the tabletop beside her as the apparition loomed up behind Gregg, knocking him aside.

Gregg turned then—turned to confront Charlie Hogan. He stood there, dazed and swaying in the gathering haze of smoke, his right hand balling into a fist that glanced weakly against the side of Gregg's jaw.

There was no time, no strength, for a second blow. Gregg closed with him, hurling him back, then smashed at his chest. Hogan dropped to his knees.

Crystal slid from the table and stood blinking through the smoke pouring down from the opening above. She saw the flailing forms as Hogan scrambled to his feet, then retreated, reeling beneath battering blows. He swung and missed while Gregg pressed forward, forcing him back to the wall. For a moment he tottered there; then Gregg's fist caught him against the left temple and he fell, sprawling amid the jars and canisters lined along the floor at the base. They clattered and rolled.

Crystal cried out and took a step forward, but Gregg was already moving in, arms outstretched, to launch himself on the body of the helpless man beneath him. As Gregg lunged forward, Hogan's hand moved out to close over one of the shining containers. Raising himself on one elbow, he hurled the jar upward with a final convulsive effort.

The glass exploded in Gregg's face in a burst of silver as

its shining contents sprayed his head and shoulders with smoking droplets that bubbled where they struck—bubbled and ate into the flesh.

With a shrill shriek, Gregg raised his hands to claw at his burning, blinded eyes, staggering back to strike heavily against the edge of the marble slab. Crystal stared at him as he stood there, haloed in smoke, his movements frozen and the shriek dying away to a gurgle deep within his throat.

Then he fell forward, and she saw the glittering shaft of the discarded scalpel wedged deeply into the base of his spine. As she watched, Gregg's body disappeared into the shroud of smoke billowing down from the hole above.

She was still standing there, shocked and stricken, when Hogan's hand gripped her arm. His voice was hoarse. "Come on!"

And then they ran.

33

THEY RAN, ran through the maze that was dark no longer, ran through the streaming smoke and down winding corridors already edged with advancing flames. There were dead ends, doors that did not open, tunnels blocked by the blaze. Twice Crystal stumbled and would have fallen, but Hogan pulled her forward at a panting run. Wheezing and choking, they reached a door at the far end of the left turning which yielded and opened to reveal the stairs leading upward.

They struggled to the landing and there, through the swirling murk, found themselves in the corridor beyond the pharmacy. Hurrying down its aisles, they halted at the front door as the fire blazed behind them.

Hogan smashed the lock and they were on the street, hastening across to the far side. Huddled in a dark doorway, they turned to stare at the burning battlements of the castle. Heads poked out of windows above them; excited voices murmured. And in the distance was the sound of galloping hooves, rumbling wheels over cobblestones. The firemen were coming.

Hogan's face was ashen, drawn. "You all right?" he murmured.

Crystal nodded, then pressed against him as her shoulders shook.

"Crissie—don't . . ." He soothed her, his voice conveying concern, then comfort. "It's all over; don't think about it anymore. We're safe, you've got your story . . ."

Crystal's sobs continued.

"That's what you wanted, right?"

She nodded, but the sobs still came, and his patience broke.

"Then stop crying, damn it!"

Crystal gulped and subsided. "Look on the bright side," Hogan said. "Jim gets his job back now. You can be married—"

"I don't want to marry Jim."

She didn't look at him, and her voice was nearly inaudible, but Hogan heard. Heard, and grinned.

"All right then, dry your eyes." He gave her his handkerchief, and as she busied herself with it, he pulled the cigar case from his vest pocket.

As he opened it, Crystal raised her face to his.

"I've been meaning to ask you something, darling," she said. Her voice was soft and sweet—and oddly firm. "Do you really have to smoke those dreadful things?"

Hogan sighed. But as he slipped the cigar case back into

his pocket, the grin returned, and he put his arm around her shoulders.

Something boomed from afar, and they looked up quickly. Perhaps the fire had reached the gas main or Gregg's stock of chemicals. If so the castle, its ogre and its victims would disappear together.

But the booming didn't come from the castle. It came from far above. Fireworks exploded against the sky, silhouetting the blazing turrets as they tottered and fell inward upon the ashes.

A single skyrocket soared, then plunged into the night.

And the Fair was over.

Postmortem

There actually was a G. Gordon Gregg.

Students of Americana may recognize him as Herman W. Mudgett, though he preferred the alliterative pseudonym of H. H. Holmes.

While certain liberties have been taken with contemporary events and his personal history, the basic facts remain. He did build a castle at Sixty-third Street and Wallace Avenue at the time of the Columbian Exposition, complete with hidden rooms, secret staircases, trapdoors and a maze of passageways. He did rent rooms to Fair visitors, and he also operated a pharmacy, posed as a physician, engaged in a wide variety of frauds and swindles, sold quack nostrums and was adept at hypnosis. If anything, his private life-style was far more fantastic than this fictional account.

The historical Holmes was apprehended, convicted and executed on homicide charges. According to his own confession, he had poisoned, asphyxiated and otherwise disposed of no fewer than twenty-seven victims.

Police investigation of the murder castle and its cellar's secrets uncovered not only the dissecting apparatus and furnace, but pits and burial places containing bones and body fragments in such chilling quantity that some officials were inclined to believe he might well have killed over two hundred.

But all this, of course, was long ago and far away. Mass murderers, gas chambers and secret burials and cold-blooded slaughter for profit belong to the dim and distant past. Today we live in more enlightened times.

Don't we?